OUT OF THE BLUE

. . . .

A Mother's Memoir

of

Our Family's Transgender Experience

. . . .

ROXANNE MOORE

PAGE PUBLISHING, INC.
New York, NY

First originally published by Page Publishing, Inc. 2017

ISBN 978-1-64027-752-6 (Paperback)
ISBN 978-1-64027-753-3 (Digital)

Printed in the United States of America

CONTENTS

PART THREE
Mother of Two Sons

For my family

With all my love

ACKNOWLEDGMENTS

Partly due to the fact that this memoir has taken so long to complete, but also because I am truly blessed to have so many supportive family, friends, and mentors (all of whom have been a part of this process in one way or another) I have many to whom I need to express my gratitude.

I know in my heart I would never have been able to see this project through to the end without the undying love and never-ending support of my husband. Thank you for every time you made me look you directly in the eye and say, "I can do this!" Especially on those days when I sincerely thought I could not. Your constant encouragement was just what I needed to help me believe in myself and my ability to tell this story the way you have always believed I could.

I am equally grateful to both of my children and my son-in-law. You and your dad are my reasons for living. Without you there would not be this story to tell. Most especially, I am thankful for my first-born child and son who willingly offered his personal writings to be part of this memoir and with whom I had more discussions than I can count in order to help me get my facts straight and to clarify any confusion I might've had about a number of things as I was in the process of writing about our family and the journey toward acceptance we've been on together. I could not have done this without your help and encouragement. I am grateful beyond words.

Other family members too have had a part in this process. Thank you to both of my sisters who are the living memory of our mother, and whose laughter and positive outlook on life I could not live without. Thank you, also, to my mother-in-law who has always been an inspiration to me by the example she sets of unconditional love and acceptance through the way she lives her life.

I also am equally grateful to have not just one, but three very close friends in my life that have each helped in their own special way throughout these past many years as I've labored on this project. Thank you, Kim, Marge, and Linda for encouraging me every step of the way. Sometimes by asking about the progress of the writing, and sometimes by remaining silent when you knew I was having a particularly hard time finding the ability or the courage to write the story. Most especially, though, thank you for being not only accepting but supportive of our unique family. Each of you is a special gift from God to me and my family.

I would be remiss if I did not take the time to also thank Donna Neal. You were there cheering me on from the start, going back to when we were office buddies and graduate teaching assistants together. You made this world a special place and you left this earth way too soon. I miss your loving, kind, and generous spirit and will always treasure the friendship we had.

I originally wrote this memoir for a creative nonfiction thesis as part of the requirements for my master's degree in English. I know I cannot thank my thesis committee members enough for the time they've taken out of their busy schedules to help see me through to the completion of this project, but I know I have to try.

Special thanks and gratitude I lovingly extend to Dr. Sandra Donaldson, my thesis committee advisor, chairperson, and impeccable editor. I'm deeply grateful that you have been on my committee from the beginning and throughout the entire process, first as a committee member and then for offering to take over as chair when my former chair relocated to another state. You could have rested on your laurels after spending a decade and a half working as chief editor on the publication of the Elizabeth Barrett Browning edition, but (being the genuinely caring and wonderful educator you are), you came to my rescue as chairperson of my committee. Thank you for your belief in the worth of this project and in my ability to complete it.

Special thanks, also, to Dr. Sharon Carson who signed on as a committee member in the beginning and stayed with me to the end, despite not seeing much progress being made for a time. Your words of encouragement, even during the stumbling blocks of this project, helped me more than you know. Thank you for advising me to take time to grieve Libby's death and for being the kind of mentor who is always encouraging and has uplifting words no matter the circumstance.

Thank you, also, Dr. David Whitcomb, for agreeing to take over as a committee member at a rather late date in the process, despite your busy schedule. Your insight and expertise as a psychologist who works with transgender individuals has been invaluable in the areas of this project that was in need of your recommendations and helpful suggestions.

Thank you, Kristin Ellwanger, for all the help and encouragement you have given me as secretary of the English Department. Many times you came to my aid and helped me a great deal by generously giving your time, advice, and/or providing answers to a number of questions I've had throughout this project.

Last, but certainly not least, my deep appreciation goes to my original thesis advisor, Dr. Libby Rankin, who insisted I write this story because she believed in the necessity of sharing it with others and in my ability to write a difficult story like this one. Although she succumbed to cancer in the early stages of this project, she has remained always with me in my mind and my heart as I've struggled to complete it. I am eternally grateful.

AUTHOR'S NOTE

When I began writing this memoir, it felt only natural and right to use everyone's actual names. Since the category of the thesis is creative nonfiction, I didn't feel it would be justifiable to use pseudonyms and still call it nonfiction. However, while I kept my real name as the writer and author, and although what is written here is nonfiction, it became increasingly clear to me as I wrote that it might not only be a good idea but necessary to use pseudonyms. Due to the extremely personal and sensitive nature of this story and in order to protect the anonymity of my other family members, I ultimately decided to change the names.

Although I don't like to dwell on it, the fact of the matter is that homophobia is alive and well, and hate crimes continue to be a problem in our society, despite the efforts of many to attain and ensure equal human rights for all. Recently, I read a *Daily News* report online that is direct proof of this. The report was about gay bashing by members of a gang from the Bronx in New York. The headline of the news article states, "Gang goes on sick rampage, sodomizing teen with plunger and forcing another to burn lover with cigarettes." Articles like this and other news reports about hate crimes are all too common. Every time I read one of these reports, it makes my heart hurt, and the fear for my children's safety resurfaces. But being aware of the common occurrence of hate crimes also serves to remind me of the importance of the work I am doing in writing this memoir. While some progress has been made toward society as a whole becoming more accepting of our gay, lesbian, bisexual, and transgender loved ones, there are still mountains to climb and many obstacles to yet overcome.

Since my children live openly and have long since come out of their respective closets, they were not overly concerned about my using their real names. However, they did agree with my decision to use pseudonyms for the reasons stated above. I asked each family member to decide what they wanted to be called, lest I choose a name they might not like for one reason or another. That made choosing names an interesting family project, and they each were careful and thoughtful in deciding on a name, some opting for names of people who hold special significance in their lives.

Other than the names, though, everything you read here is true to the best of my knowledge. However, it is *my* written version of the truth based on letters, journal entries, and mostly my memory. The way we remember things, even the things we remember about specific events, can and often do vary from one person to another who have experienced the same event. Our memories are, in fact, our personally created version of what we believe to be the truth.

I have made the authorial decision to write most of the story reflectively, as opposed to using a lot of scene and dialogue, in my attempt to demonstrate my interest in memory and authentic voice. Looking back on things that have happened since my first child was born, I then probe those experiences to try and make some sense of it all in the present day, not just for myself but for the reader as well. To paraphrase memoirist Patricia Hampl, I wrote this memoir not just to relate what I think I know, but to attempt to discover what it is that I don't know.

INTRODUCTION

The indisputable facts about me and my family are this. I am a sixty-year-old woman raised as a Catholic in a small town in conservative western North Dakota. As a young girl, I was sure I wanted to become a nun. Then I met my husband, Aaron. He is the love of my life and my best friend, and a couple of months ago we celebrated our fortieth wedding anniversary. We have lived in a college town in the eastern part of the state for most of our married life, where I have been primarily a stay-at-home mom, who decided at the age of 46 (once both our children left home) to return to college to work toward a degree in English. My husband, Aaron, upon graduating from medical school and completing his residency, has worked as a family physician for most of our married life and supported our family well.

We have two adult children, both of whom I love more than life itself and always will. Our firstborn child, Tommie, is thirty-nine years old, and my baby, Henry, is thirty-four. This is where the indisputable facts about my life and family become a bit hazier and, for most of the people I've met, difficult to comprehend. Until a few years ago, I could always say with certainty that my husband and I had one girl and one boy. I can no longer say that, even though that's how I gave birth.

The following memoir, while it is our family's story, centers mainly on our older child and me. I've tried to describe what it's been like coming to terms with the knowledge that the baby girl I gave birth to in 1971 and named Catherine Michelle legally changed her name to Tommie Michele in 2004 and now identifies as a man.

There have been countless times in the past few years, as I've been working on this memoir, that I've sat at my desk in my office staring at an empty computer screen wishing I had a profound way of telling this story, and describing my feelings about the difficulties I've had trying to tell it. The trouble is I don't. It's not that I don't believe it's an important story. On the contrary, not only do I realize its importance, I believe it's one that *needs* to be told. However, in part because of the perfectionist tendencies in my makeup, one of the problems I've encountered while trying to write the memoir that follows is my inability to believe I'm capable of writing something this important in a way that will not only interest but captivate a reader. Believe me, perfectionism is a curse—not a blessing— especially in this case.

But it's not only my lack of confidence that has been such a stumbling block. For one thing, it's a confusing story. I believe I've reached the point where I understand things more clearly, but it's another thing to attempt writing it down in a way that will help others see more clearly what it means to the parent of a transgender child. Furthermore, I've had to force myself to go back and relive the experience of first finding out then coping with the idea, trying to understand and ultimately accepting that my first child, who was born a baby girl, now identifies and lives his life as an adult man.

Going back to that confusing and sometimes painful time in my life and the lives of the other members of our family is not something I've enjoyed, but in order to tell the story this is what I've had to force myself to do. I, along with the rest of the family, have overcome those initial hurdles, and we're in a good place in our lives now, having come to embrace Tommie as a female-to-male (FTM) transgender person. So I've agonized over having to transport myself back to that time and place when I first began to realize what my daughter's feelings were about her gender identity and her intention to change from a female to a male when she realized it was possible to do so.

Most of the time, I tell myself I'm just not capable of writing the story, and yet I've still felt compelled to continue trying. It's been a constant struggle between the part of me that wants to just enjoy my family and live in the moment and the part of me that realizes the importance of sharing our unique story with others. Though the story does not focus on Henry, our younger son, I think it's important to let the reader know at the outset that he is gay and has been in a committed relationship with Joe for five years. So the gay, lesbian, bi-sexual, and transgender (GLBT) community holds special significance for me and my family. Our story could serve not only to educate and promote awareness but possibly lead to a better understanding and acceptance of our GLBT loved ones. That is my hope and my prayer. So I've forced myself to continue writing.

But again I ask myself, how do I even begin to tell this story? Do I start at the beginning, and if so, what *is* the beginning? Perhaps more importantly, what is the real truth? Trying to answer these seemingly simple questions has been the bane of my existence for the past five years. Of course, there have been a multitude of questions I've needed to address as a result of this work, but I've decided it's probably best to take those as they come and try to keep the story as simple as possible for now.

One thing I will say is that since Tommie began his transition and throughout the process of the transformation of our family, I have come to the conclusion that there might not even *be* such a thing as an indisputable fact. Never once, in my wildest imagination, would I have thought when my daughter was born that she would someday become my son. But that is what has happened and that is the reality my family and I now live with.

So I sit here at my desk at this moment surrounded by several fragmentary rough drafts, trying to decide how to piece them together into a cohesive whole. On the bookshelves and scattered in various places on my desk and in other areas of my home office are a multitude of memoirs I have read that have been written and published by other transgender people. However, so far, I have been able to find only a handful of works written by a parent of a transgender person, although I've searched diligently for more. One of the works is a memoir by feminist writer, teacher, and poet Hilda Raz written in conjunction with her female-to-male transgender son, titled *What Becomes You.* The book was given to me as a Mother's Day gift from Tommie in 2008. He wrote an inscription at the back, which says in part, "I imagine you finding familiar feelings expressed in these pages, as I did. His story is not my story but there's resonance for me in it – in the chorus of T voices, I find harmony. In the mother's words too. Having been your daughter, having never been ashamed of that, now growing from the privilege of being your son, I am blessed to be your child always, your blood in my veins, your love surrounds me."

In the mother's section of the memoir, Hilda Raz expresses some of the exact sentiments that I have felt while trying to write my memoir. She says,

> **I wonder how best to tell my story, to blend it with my son's, which is not only the story of his body. I, too, have come to understand that I am not only my body. What I have to tell is located in the relationship between a parent and her child. It is true to the best of my knowledge. But**

nonfiction uses some of the techniques of fiction. Readers will and should assume our stories are true. But part of the truth is that for thirty years what seemed an irrefutable fact – I was present and saw myself give birth to a daughter – turns out to be fiction. (Raz, 230)

These words could just as well be mine because our stories are so similar in nature. I even made that exact comment in the margin the first time I read that passage. We are both mothers of FTM transgender children, with both our children being in their early thirties before beginning their transition, and we both are concerned about how best to tell the story, mainly because we recognize the importance of getting it right—of telling a story our readers can relate to and understand.

In addition to Tommie's inscription in the book, there is also a portion of another essay he wrote that is included as part of one of the chapters. Also, there are two other original writings written by my child that have been added as appendices. I feel it's important to include some of Tommie's writings as part of this memoir in order for the reader to be able to see some things from his perspective as the child being written about. The meditations written by Tommie over the past decade (from 1996 to 2007) are an important display of the consistency of his core values while in the midst of the major life changes he was undergoing. In that respect, I suppose you could say this work is also somewhat of a collaboration as well between my child and myself.

As I said earlier, though, it has been a rare occurrence to find things written by parents or other loved ones on this topic. I recently discovered a book by the mother of a male to female transgender person titled *Mom, I Need to Be a Girl*. The only other nonfiction work I'm aware of written by family members of the transgender person is a book titled *Transforming Families: Real Stories About Transgendered Loved Ones,* edited by Mary Boenke. As opposed to a memoir, it is an anthology of short stories and essays written by various parents.

While the memoirs written by transgender persons have been helpful for me in gaining insight into my child's experience, the above-mentioned anthology and Hilda Raz's section of the memoir have been more helpful to me because the stories are written from the parent's perspective. That perspective, the one of a parent, is the one from which I've tried to present the following story.

PROLOGUE

It's a Reality!

January, 2007 – When I look at Tommie, I still see Cathy. She was my firstborn and my daughter for over thirty years before she became my son, so this transition is not something that's been easy for me.

Apparently other people who don't know Tommie or that he was born female have been seeing a male when they look at Tommie for quite some time now. I've experienced people seeing him this way on occasion recently when being out in public with him. Strangers immediately recognize Tommie as a "he," and I have to be careful to use the correct pronouns when referring to him, so as not to give him away. I'm working on it, and over time it gets easier and rolls off the tongue more easily. But I still miss Cathy.

♦   ♦   ♦

June, 2006 – Aaron has just recently returned from the East Coast where he attended the wedding of our niece. Tommie and his wife, Francine, went with him to the wedding while I stayed behind because of school commitments. I'm anxious to see the pictures so my husband makes it a priority to download them onto the computer from our digital camera. I sit down to look at the pictures, and the first one I see makes my heart start beating in double-time. I'm shaken to the core by the first picture I see of Tommie. I look at it more closely, and then I scan quickly through the rest of the pictures, hoping I wasn't seeing things right . . . that maybe on that first picture what looked to me like facial hair might have just been a shadow or something. I look up at Aaron who is standing there watching me as I look at the pictures. "Please tell me that's not what I think it is." But he just smiles at me and shrugs his shoulders. All the pictures I'm seeing of Tommie confirm it. He now has a small goatee on the point of his chin. Although it's not the full-grown beard I've been dreading ever since he first began transitioning, it's facial hair that is meant to be seen and used to identify Tommie as a person of the male gender.

◆　　◆　　◆

How do I describe the feelings of loss and sadness that seeing these pictures have caused me? Immediately following the sadness, however, come those of remorse and shame, because I thought I was well on my way toward accepting Tommie's transgender identity. But seeing Tommie with facial hair has made me realize I still have a way to go and lots more work to do.

My logical mind tells me that, of course, this is Tommie's way of taking away any doubt in other people's minds, including his mother's, as to what gender he is. My aching heart, however, longs for the daughter I now am beginning to realize I've lost forever. She's been fading away into the past for quite some time now. Over a decade ago, when she first came out as a lesbian, she quit shaving her legs and under her arms. It's an aspect of our Western culture she said she disagreed with. I thought she was being lazy and was using a political view to condone the laziness and I told her so. Although the leg and underarm hair bothered me for quite a while, I learned over time to live with it and even accept it. But I will also admit, now that Tommie identifies as a male, the body and leg hair seem more acceptable to me. Societal norms are more ingrained in our minds than we sometimes think they are. Society says it is normal for males to sport body hair.

Once our children became adults, some of their decisions haven't met with my and my husband's approval as parents, but there's not much we could do about it. God knows I've learned that lesson over and over again in the past several years. Aaron, however, has not had as much difficulty simply accepting things as they are, so he's been an anchor for me as well as a good role model. I'm not entirely sure why, but I suspect it's because of his natural tendency to be an easy-going and very open-minded person. I always thought I was too, but I didn't like it when I learned Tommie had been given the go-ahead by his therapist to begin hormone therapy either. However, that idea was something I could choose to either think about or not. I chose not to seriously think about it and tried to pretend it wasn't happening. Despite the fact that his voice began to deepen because of the hormones he had begun to take, it sounded to me like he just had a bad cold, and that's the way I chose to deal with his deeper male voice, at least in the beginning. So why is something seemingly as trivial as this little bit of facial hair so disturbing to me, especially since he is well into the process of transitioning from female to male? The only logical answer I have is because the facial hair has made it clearer to me than anything else that this is real. It's not just something to talk about theoretically or choose to avoid or chalk up to some other reason. It's such an obvious *visual* confirmation of my daughter becoming my son, and I realize more than ever the harsh reality of it all.

PART ONE

Mother of One Girl, One Boy

CHAPTER ONE

Beyond the Confessional

I often refer to myself as a *recovering Catholic* and invariably the reaction to such a statement is at least a smile, sometimes a giggle, and then there are times that whoever I am talking to will come right out and laugh. I'm not sure why people think it's funny. I think it's a little sad. I'll be the first to admit that I sometimes miss the reassuring comfort that came with the strong convictions of faith I had while growing up. I was born and raised a Catholic, and for many years (even in my young adult life while we were raising our two children) I found no reason to question any of the tenets of the Catholic Church.

But that was a long time ago, and several things have happened in my life and the lives of those I hold most dear that have caused me to stop and not only think about but question some of the things I was taught. As for the laws of the Catholic faith that I followed so unwaveringly while growing up, I now have many doubts and questions about those as well. Unfortunately, most of those questions have no answers that are compatible with what I now firmly believe with all my heart and soul to be true. So I refer to myself as a *recovering* Catholic. "Bless me, Father, for I have sinned," I used to say at the beginning of each weekly confession. As my story unfolds, maybe you'll come to understand why this is one of the church sacraments I no longer avail myself of.

I do, however, believe in God. I can even say with firm conviction that my faith in God is stronger than it ever was. However, I see my God as a loving God, and throughout the struggles of the past several years, I've held on to the knowledge that His most basic command to us is to "Love one another, as I have loved you."

Therefore, one thing that I have never (nor will I ever) question is that I love both of my children, and I know my children love me. Furthermore, and perhaps more importantly, I also know that God loves us all—no matter what the Catholic Church or *some* right-wing Christians say about what is right and what is wrong. This is a thought that has sustained me throughout all the struggles of the transformation of our family.

This doesn't make the story any easier to relate to, though. There's so much to tell. So much I want to share with others who might be on the same path as I am and even with those who aren't because I believe it's an important story. Some of it you will probably find confusing. I know I'm still confused about a lot of things, and I'm the one living it. So I decided that maybe if I put it all down on paper I'll be able to work out some of the confusion and even some of the doubts I still have that have been rumbling around in my head and my heart for the past few years. I'm sure it can't hurt to try. Hold on to your hat, though. It's going to be a roller coaster of a ride.

CHAPTER TWO

Is it a Boy or a Girl?

As I've been struggling with how to begin my story, the following thought came to me. Our oldest child has been married twice. The first time, she married a man. The second time, he married a woman.

Yes, I'm talking about the same person. The first time she was the bride, and I thought she looked beautiful in her wedding dress. Her father and I walked her down the aisle and were as happy as most parents are when their child gets married. But the first marriage did not last—probably because (as we now know) it wasn't ever meant to last. Five years ago, he was the groom and he wore a tuxedo. In my admittedly prejudiced opinion as the mother of the groom, I thought he looked quite handsome. Once again, my husband and I walked him down the aisle together—this time feeling just as much joy—along with some apprehension and the hope that he'd finally found true happiness. Tommie and his wife will soon celebrate their sixth wedding anniversary, and I'm happy for them and the love they share. I hope and pray that their marriage will last a lifetime, and I'm confident that this is their intention as well.

But I've become leery of the so-called happy ending. The familiar line from the fairy tales "and they all lived happily ever after" is just that, I think. A fairy tale. At least that's what experience has led me to believe. I am not saying this specifically about my child's marriage. It has more to do with what has happened historically in the family I grew up in when it comes to marriage. In my family, the divorce rate among my siblings exceeds the national average. Of the five children my parents had, only two of us have been lucky enough to find and fall in love with the right person the first time and remain married to that person to this day. As for my daughter and my sibling's children, most of their marriages have failed in the first couple of years. So basically, I've come to develop a rather jaded feeling about marriage and happy endings in general.

Besides that, though, I've also learned that life is truly a series of ups and downs. Along with happiness there often comes sadness, and I know this is true of everyone's life. Why else would traditional wedding vows state that you will stay by each other through the good times and the bad, in sickness and in health?

I used to think that the ups and downs started shortly after our daughter's first marriage. But I've come to the realization recently that it would be more honest to admit that it all began the day she was born. The serious turmoil and doubts that I referred to as a roller coaster ride didn't start until after she got married but still, the day she came into being is the day both my life and my husband's changed completely forever. Ask any parent, and I have no doubt they'd probably agree that the birth of their first child is definitely one of the most dramatic life-changing events of one's life.

When I found out I was pregnant, my reaction was a combination of fear and excitement. Basically, we were still newlyweds. We hadn't even been married for a year. My husband was only a junior in college, and the plan was for him to attend medical school after graduating. Money was extremely scarce, and I knew this would only add to the financial bind we were already in. As easily as I got pregnant, we later would look back in hindsight and realize I should probably have taken the birth-control pill from the beginning. However, being the practicing Catholics we were, we started out our marriage by using the rhythm method, which was the only kind of birth control the Catholic Church condoned in the early 1970s. Today we joke about it and tell people it's because she was a rhythm baby that our daughter possesses a great musical ability. But our son Henry is also very musically inclined, and we abandoned the rhythm method of birth control after I got pregnant the first time.

I gave birth to a baby girl just eight days before my twenty-first birthday. She put up quite the struggle to be born. I was in labor with her for twenty-five hours, and perhaps that should have given me an inkling of what was to come in future years. In spite of the difficulty I had bringing her into this world, friends and family commented about what a great birthday present she was. Naturally, I agreed, but I also have to admit that it wasn't all happiness and joy, at least not for me personally. At the time, I thought maybe it was partly because I was so young and also because money was so tight for my husband and me that I wasn't totally ecstatic about everything. Years later, I would be able to recognize with the help of my physician that postpartum depression was the main cause for the many tears I shed those first few months. Along with the tears came a tremendous feeling of guilt. Why wasn't I completely and totally happy?

At least part of the guilt, I think, came from something my mother told me once when we were talking about having babies. She gave birth to five children, so I figured she probably knew what she was talking about. She told me that even though giving birth was a painful process, the minute she held her newborn baby in her arms she totally forgot about the pain she'd endured to have it. This was definitely not the case with me. In fact, it was on the delivery table that I decided to start taking the birth-control pill. I didn't care that the Catholic Church didn't condone it; I didn't want to have to go through that again for a long time. When it was over and I held my baby girl in my arms I was happy, but I did not have that overwhelming feeling of joy that helped alleviate all the pain. Mainly, I was just glad I'd survived the ordeal of childbirth. I thought either my mother had lied to me or, worse yet, that maybe this was an indication that I wasn't going to be a very good mother.

We named her Catherine Michelle; she was not only our first child, but she was also the first grandchild born into both of our families. Since she remained the only grandchild for five years, she got lots of extra attention and presents, as I'm sure you can well imagine. She had tons of little baby dresses, many more than she could ever wear out.

Most of us called her Cathy. My dad, however, came up with the special and more unique nickname of Madame Queen, because, he explained, "That little one is definitely the ruler of her own universe." Of course we couldn't have known at the time how meaningful those words of explanation would turn out to be.

There's an experience I remember when she was only a few months old that made me a little angry when it happened. I used to dress her in pink a lot because she didn't have a lot of hair as a baby. But she did have lots of little pink dresses and outfits, and I always figured as long as I dressed her in pink there would never be any confusion about the fact that she was a little girl, despite her lack of hair. After all, isn't the color we dress our babies in one of the many ways our society displays to the public what gender our children are? They start the practice immediately after a baby's birth in the hospital nurseries, or at least they did when I gave birth. When Cathy was born, it was pink blankets and knitted hats for girl babies, and blue ones for boys. Interestingly, however, neither of the two little dresses that my husband bought for her the day she was born was pink. One was yellow and the other was lime green. We dressed her in the yellow one the day we brought her home from the hospital. She had a dark complexion, and the color yellow looked so pretty on her. But the clothes she got from other people were all pink so she wore a lot of pink—at least in that first year. That's why I was so shocked the day someone questioned my baby's gender.

◆ ◆ ◆

It is early summer. I'm standing in the checkout line at Kmart (with Cathy in the cart in her baby carrier) when the lady in front of me looks at her and smiles. "Oh, what a cute little baby!" she says. "Thanks," I reply with no small amount of pride. But those feelings are fleeting as she follows the compliment by asking, "Is it a boy or a girl?" I am completely insulted. I inform her: "She's a girl" while stifling the urge to make a snotty remark. In my mind I wonder how she could even ask such a question. Would a baby boy be dressed in pink from head to toe, for heaven's sake?

◆ ◆ ◆

I was very happy when her hair finally grew out, and yes, she wore it long and in pigtails for several years while growing up.

I'm not sure why this memory is still so vivid in my mind. But it is. I can remember it as clearly as if it had happened yesterday. My husband, after reading an early draft of this memoir, asked me, "Did this really happen?" Maybe he thought it was an act of poetic license and that I'd made the story up for dramatic effect. My reply to my husband's question was "Yes, honey, it really happened! Isn't it interesting considering what we know now?"

It's not just how well this particular memory fits into the story I'm telling that amazes me, but that I can still remember it so clearly. But maybe I shouldn't be so surprised. I'm thinking of some words about memory from noted memoirist Patricia Hampl. In her essay "Memory and Imagination" from her book *I Could Tell You Stories* she says:

> **We store in memory only images of value. The value may be lost over the passage of time, but that's the implacable judgment of feeling: This, we say somewhere within us, is something I'm hanging on to. And, of course, often we cleave to things because they possess heavy negative charges. Pain has strong arms. (p. 29)**

I don't think I held on to this memory because of any physical pain inflicted upon me by a stranger's innocent question. But it certainly bothered me a great deal that she couldn't tell if my baby was a boy or a girl. What I'm trying to understand at this point in my life is, "Why did that matter so much to me?" As a young mother, had I unconsciously wished more for a baby girl than a boy? Perhaps. Is the fact that I still remember the incident so clearly now an indication of the pain I've felt in losing my daughter? I suspect that might be part of it.

Cathy was our only child for five years. When she was three years old, I got pregnant again but lost it due to a miscarriage. The doctor told us it was "God's way of taking care of something that should've never been." At the time, I accepted what I suppose were meant to be a doctor's reassuring words to a grieving mother and didn't even ask any questions. I never got to see it, never got to hold it, much less have a funeral and bury it as they do now with babies that aren't full term. Years later, I came to regret that I didn't insist on at least seeing and holding the baby, but this was the early 1970s and things like that just weren't done in those days, I guess.

As I sit here today writing this story I wish more than ever that we had at least asked whether it was a boy or a girl. I have to admit that in the recesses of my heart, I'm hoping it was a girl. Maybe it's because of what's happened that this is now important to me, but I'm still struggling with why that is. Some mothers never get to experience having a daughter at all. Why, then, don't I just feel lucky to at least have had the experience?

Two years after my miscarriage our son was born. We named him Henry Aaron after his dad, and I called him "my little peanut." On one of my favorite pictures of him as a baby, his little face is oval and all scrunched up and he looks just like a little peanut. At any rate, my husband and I were glad that we were lucky enough to have *one of each.* That fit especially nice into what my sense of order was in those days. One girl, one boy, so we decided to be done having children and concentrate on raising the two healthy children God had given us.

To be completely honest, though, it wasn't just the fact that we had one child of each gender that made us decide to be done having children. The postpartum depression that I somehow was able to survive after giving birth to each of my children was frightening for both my husband and me. We decided it would be best not to tempt fate by trying to have more children. I wasn't sure I could survive another episode. I was absolutely positive I didn't want to find out.

CHAPTER THREE

"No, Mommy, I Want to Wear my *Real* Clothes!"

Cathy has always had a strong mind of her own, even as a young child. As soon as she was old enough to speak, the simple act of getting dressed became a challenge. I would try to convince her to wear one of the many dresses she always had, and she would toss them aside, pick her blue jeans and T-shirt out of the drawer, and hold them up to me, exclaiming, "No, Mommy! I wanna wear my *real* clothes." I suppose by real clothes, she might have meant they were more comfortable. I can't deny the fact that I have always preferred wearing casual clothes (like jeans or slacks or—better yet—sweats) instead of a dress myself. Wouldn't most women, now that we've been liberated? As she got older I remember that our trips together to buy new clothes for school were never the kind of joyful bonding events that I always wished they could be. In fact, it usually ended badly with us getting in fights. She always hated the clothes I would pick out for her and wanted instead the kinds of clothes that I always thought were ugly on her. I can't help but wonder, now, if she wasn't trying to express her gender identity from the time she was a little girl.

◆　◆　◆

I have the desire, here, to want to just skip over my daughter's growing-up years completely because it doesn't seem to me like an important part of the story I want to tell. Furthermore, I wonder whether anyone will even be interested in reading about these years because it was all so normal.

But maybe that's precisely why I've decided I can't just completely ignore those years. Their very normalcy, I suppose, is one of the reasons I have for writing my story. I want to try to dispel most people's notion that a person who identifies as transgender is somehow not normal or some kind of freak of nature. That they just drop out of the sky one day and don't come from "families."

◆　◆　◆

I'll be the first to admit that Cathy was, without a doubt, a tomboy. Our society uses that term to describe little girls who prefer activities little boys like and toys or other items that are normally regarded as only being for little boys. Dolls for girls, trucks for boys, right? Although I never pulled a snake out of Cathy's pocket (thank God!) she loved bugs and frogs and animals of all kinds and would have kept them as pets if I'd allowed her to. In fact, there was a period of a couple of days when she was a little girl that she did just that.

◆　◆　◆

Cathy is six years old, and Henry is only one and a half, and we are on a family vacation at a lake resort where there are no televisions, no telephones in the cabins. We have specifically chosen this kind of vacation because Aaron is a resident in medical school, and we decide a week on a lake in the woods will be a relaxing change for all of us. Cathy captures a couple of tiny tree frogs and makes a little nest for them out of grass and leaves in a small pencil box she's brought along for her crayons. She names them Albert and Marvin and for a period of two or three days they're all she is interested in playing with. I think to myself as I watch her taking care of these little tree frogs what a nurturing little mommy she is being. Then, a few days later, she spots a bigger tree frog. She catches it and puts it in the nest with the baby ones. She doesn't name that one, though. In the morning when she wakes up, the two little baby tree frogs are dead. It completely ruins her vacation and puts a damper on ours as well. She cries and cries and keeps blaming herself for killing Albert and Marvin. "It's all my fault, Mommy! I killed them!" We have an emotional burial for them by the cabin, and she sets the big frog free.

On our way home after the vacation, she's sobbing out loud in the car and keeps repeating through her tears "If only I wouldn't have put that dumb big frog in with Albert and Marvin, they would still be alive!" I feel so utterly helpless not being able to do or say anything that might make her feel better. All I can do is dry her tears, put my arms around her, and love her and hope she'll soon be able to forget.

◆　◆　◆

She's never forgotten about it, though, and neither have I. On another vacation a couple of years later in Florida, she's fascinated by the small tree lizards that are everywhere around the grounds of the hotel where we are staying. She takes sticks and plays with them while her little brother and I swim in the pool nearby. These, however, I do not allow her to keep as pets for any length of time.

It's not that she didn't have dolls to play with. She had her share of Barbie dolls and other ones too, but it was her huge stuffed animal collection that she treasured more than anything. She treated them like her children.

During her junior and senior high school years, she was extremely active in extracurricular activities. She began participating in various school sports such as track and basketball, which kept her busy enough, but she was also involved in music activities like choir and band. She was a very bright student and always got high grades on her report cards. At parent/teacher conferences, we never received anything less than glowing reports from all of her teachers.

When she became old enough to date, she had her share of boyfriends, and they took her to the high school proms and dances and out on other dates while her girlfriends went out with their boyfriends. So you see, it was all very normal—whatever that means.

The one thing that I sometimes got frustrated about, though, is how much she cared for her friends that were girls. Even after she started dating and had boyfriends, it was the girls that were her friends that she sometimes went out of her way to please.

One time I remember not only being frustrated but getting extremely angry with her because it seemed (at least to me) she had gone completely overboard to show her best friend how much she liked her. I had given her money to buy an outfit for a special occasion that was coming up. Her friend went with her to shop for the outfit, but when she got home she was empty-handed. When I asked her why she hadn't bought anything she simply explained to me that she'd spent it on an outfit for her friend instead. "She really wanted it, Mom. And she didn't have any money to buy it, so I got it for her. Besides, I don't really need a new outfit anyway and it really made her happy!"

It may have made her friend happy, but it made me very angry. Partly, because it seemed to me that her friends never seemed to reciprocate and I thought Cathy was just "too good" of a friend and told her so on more than one occasion.

Those words would come back to haunt me years later, though, when she said in her coming-out letter to us: "It took me twenty two years to get through denial, confusion, and self-hatred about who I am. Not just about my sexuality but so many things about myself. Like being ashamed of being 'too good of a friend' when people are goddamn lucky that friends like me exist."

Some might say that the fact she was a tomboy—that she liked bugs, hated dresses, and enjoyed sports—were indications of what was to come. I won't deny that we certainly thought back on all of this when she came out to us. But lots of little girls have these same likes and dislikes—both heterosexuals and homosexuals alike. All of Cathy's friends were very much like her; but most of them are married to men, now, and are having children of their own. Besides, it's one thing to look back in retrospect and recognize it. It's a completely different thing in a society such as ours to see things at the time and realize what's going on.

Maybe we are blinded in many ways by what Adrienne Rich calls compulsory heterosexuality. I know that in the conservative, rural Midwest where we live it is common to automatically assume that everyone around us is heterosexual. That's not the case, of course, but it's what we tend to think. Until we are confronted with homosexuality in our very own family, many of us allow ourselves to believe that everyone is heterosexual. After their child has "come out" to them, some parents will say that they always secretly suspected their child was gay and weren't even surprised when their child finally came out. What I have noticed, however, is that these are usually the parents of a gay man. For reasons I'm unable to explain we seem to accept it much more readily when our little girls exhibit the behaviors of a tomboy. Is it possibly because of our male-dominated society that we still live in that most of us are not as alarmed when a little girl exhibits male behavior? Could that also be why it is seen as a much more negative and alarming thing when our little boys exhibit what society calls girlish or girly behavior? I don't have definitive answers to those questions. I am aware, though, that there is scientific research that supports my theories, but I have not yet taken the time to actually read these studies. I also know my husband and I were taken totally by surprise, and I will even say we were shocked when our daughter began questioning her sexual orientation shortly after she got married the first time. Thus began the transformation of our family that is an ongoing process to this day.

CHAPTER FOUR

The First Wedding

The summer after she graduated from high school, Cathy went to work at a summer resort much like the resort we've spent our one-week summer vacations all the while she was growing up. Being a guest at a summer resort had put it in her mind that a summertime dream job would be to work at one of these resorts.

That's where she met Bob, the man she would marry just three years later. Our first impression of Bob wasn't the most positive one as he drove a motorcycle, and my husband and I didn't relish the idea of him tearing around the countryside with Cathy on the back. But once we got to know Bob, we liked him a lot, and it wasn't too long before we considered him part of the family. Bob and Henry got along great too, so we looked at him as the brother our son had never had. Henry was going through the difficult teenage years, and it was a comfort to me that Bob seemed to relate to him so well.

But we weren't all that excited when Cathy and Bob announced that they wanted to get married. They set the date, and the wedding preparations began. I wasn't prepared to be a "mother of the bride" just yet, and I struggled with the idea of the two of them getting married so young, despite the fact that Cathy was older than I was when Aaron and I got married.

When I watch those "Bridezilla" shows on television, I think back to when Cathy and I were planning her first wedding, and I have to admit I was a full-blown "Motherzilla." To try and alleviate all the hassles of wedding planning, at one point my husband and I offered the two of them money for a nice honeymoon or something in lieu of having a big wedding, but they wanted the big wedding ceremony with a reception, dinner, and dance to celebrate with friends and family.

Somehow we got through all the ups and downs of wedding planning, and they got married in June at the Catholic Church where we were members. It was a great wedding, and in the end, I decided it had been worth all the effort it took to plan it. Cathy had learned to play guitar and write her own music, and she wrote a song that she sang for Bob at the wedding that was especially touching. Bob asked Henry to be a groomsman at the wedding, and I think Henry felt really honored. Three days later, I wrote the following in my journal:

> June 30 – My daughter was married three days ago and my heart was so full of joy that I found it difficult to cry tears of sadness. As I stood in the front row of the church watching and listening to her vow her life to Bob I remembered how happy I was when I married Aaron twenty- two years ago. I have prayed since my daughter was born that she would grow up to find true love and happiness. How can a parent be sad when their most fervent prayer has been answered? . . . And now we have a new member in our family who has already brought us so much joy. Our son finally has the brother he's always wanted.

I'm sitting here now looking at this journal entry and can vaguely recall how happy I was during that time. But I also can recognize these many years later after all I've learned from what we've gone through that I was making assumptions based on how *I* was feeling at the time. Was my daughter truly that happy? Had she actually found true love? It certainly seemed so to me, but was I just projecting my own feelings onto my daughter and her new husband? My son had never really expressed to us in so many words that he wanted a brother. Why did I even write that? Was it maybe that *I* regretted not having more children and therefore thought that's what my son wanted too?

Because of what has transpired in our family in the eighteen years since my daughter's first marriage, I can look back now and realize with much more clarity that I unwittingly projected a lot of my own feelings onto my daughter and my son not just while they were growing up but into their early adult lives as well. If I was happy, then surely they must be happy too, right? In the years since, I've learned how important it is for me not to do that to my children and to at least try to be more attentive to what their needs and desires are as opposed to just mine.

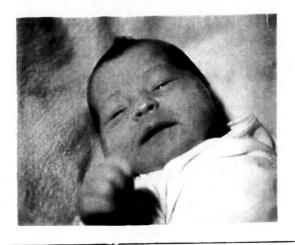

1971 - Catherine Michelle
(1 day old)

1971 - Cathy - 6 mos.

1972 - Cathy - 1 year
and Aaron

1973 - Cathy - Age 2 yrs.

1974 - Cathy - Age 3
"Third Birthday"

1976 - Cathy - Age 5

1976 - Cathy Age 5 with
Henry 2 mos. old

Cathy - 7 yrs old
Henry - 2 yrs old

Miami, Florida
Me with Cathy - age 10
and Henry Age 5

At the Lake
Cathy - Age 13   Henry - Age 8

Niagara Falls 1984
Cathy - Age 15   Heny Age 10
& Aaron

Cathy - "Sweet 16"

PART TWO

Mother of Lesbian Daughter and Teenage Son

CHAPTER FIVE

"Should We Tell Her?"

A trip I took from Grand Forks to Duluth one weekend in April not even a year after my daughter was married turned out to be much more significant than I could have ever expected. I was going to Duluth to help her and her husband move into a different apartment, and though the ride isn't a particularly long one, I certainly had time during the drive to think about the possibilities the weekend might bring. It was springtime, and new life was budding everywhere, which probably contributed to my feeling so happy and hopeful about the weekend. While driving I recalled the rhyme we recited when I was growing up. "First comes love, then comes marriage, then comes Cathy with a baby carriage!" At that time, I still believed that was the normal progression of life.

They'd told me they were moving because they needed more space. An extra bedroom, perhaps? I hadn't been outwardly urging them to start a family, but I'll admit I had the notion that I would become a grandmother, now that Cathy was married.

I did receive announcements from them that weekend. The first filled me with momentary excitement.

◆ ◆ ◆

It is midmorning and we are in the living room, waiting for the muffins Cathy is making for brunch to finish baking. The apartment is filled with the aroma of blueberry muffins, and empty boxes are scattered throughout, waiting to be filled for the move. My son-in-law asks Cathy, "Should we tell her?" My daughter just looks at me and grins a little sheepishly. Here it comes, I think to myself; they're going to tell me they're expecting a baby. My hopes are quickly dashed, however, when they lead me to the window and show me a car Bob has just bought, sitting across the street. Bob's dream car, Cathy says. It's an old-model Oldsmobile he's always wanted. A classic, I think he says it is, but for me, a potential grandchild has just become an ugly, mustard-yellow car. So much for that dream—for now—anyway.

◆ ◆ ◆

A little later I was confronted with another announcement, in retrospect a much weightier one, though I didn't recognize that at the time. We were in the kitchen doing dishes after brunch. This was rare, since Cathy was not much of a homemaker—at least she never seemed interested in cooking. Usually, when we went to visit, my husband and I took them out to eat. But we had a strenuous day of packing and moving ahead of us, so she made it a point to begin by making brunch. When we started doing dishes, I was feeling a bit of satisfaction that Cathy was beginning to take her life as a married woman more seriously. I was also a little concerned about her, though. Earlier, while she'd been busy in the kitchen preparing the brunch, I'd begun packing some boxes and noticed a card she'd received from her best friend displayed on the dresser. Since Cathy usually shared things like this with me, I didn't think anything of picking up the card to read the verse on the inside. However, the handwritten note from her friend on the inside of the card was unsettling to me. She said she knew Cathy was going through a confusing time, and dealing with some scary things, and said she would pray for her.

I decided to try and find out what her friend had meant, so while we were doing dishes, I said, "Sooo, Cathy, I saw the card you got from Jenny. What's so confusing and scary?" Her response, as it turns out, was the second announcement that day. Hesitating a bit, standing back from the sink, she looked at me then out the window and said, "Well, Mom, I wasn't really planning to tell you this yet, but … I think I might be bisexual." She said it rather casually and then she quickly added, "But it's not that I don't love Bob anymore, though, because I do!" Her reassurance came so quick, after what I now believe to be the beginning of her questioning her sexual orientation, that I felt it wasn't a big deal. She was in college, majoring in psychology and women's studies, and she often delved into philosophical issues I sometimes didn't understand. I was aware of the word "bisexual," but the concept of it wasn't something I gave much consideration to. I saw myself as an open-minded mother and was proud of that. So keeping my cool, I said calmly and slowly, "Well, if you think about it, Cathy—isn't everyone bisexual to a certain degree? I mean, I love Daddy with all my heart. But I also love my best friend. It's just that my love for her isn't in any way sexual."

I added my opinion that just because she had some deep feelings for some of her female friends, that didn't necessarily mean she was bisexual, did it? We then had a long conversation about bisexuality. I realize now I wasn't paying attention to what I was hearing. I'm pretty sure I didn't want to pay attention. I downplayed the significance of the conversation, and more or less dismissed it from my mind.

But that night, lying in my makeshift bed in their apartment in Duluth after a long and tiring day, I remembered my morning conversation with Cathy. *Bisexual*, she had said. That word still bothered me, but she'd reassured me she still loved Bob and that helped a little. My hopes of becoming a grandmother might be delayed but weren't dashed completely. I wished that Aaron was there with me to cuddle up to for reassurance, but he wasn't, so the possibility of someday becoming a grandmother were the thoughts I clung to for comfort as I drifted off to sleep.

◆　◆　◆

That weekend was the beginning of some valuable lessons that I'm continuing to learn even as I sit here writing. One thing I do know for certain by now and have realized from experiences with my daughter and my son is that every time I declared with conviction as they were growing up that all I wanted was for them to be happy, what I really meant (without even being aware of it) was that I wanted them to make *me* happy. I will often hear parents of young children express that very thing in conversation: "All we want is for our children to grow up and be happy." I always have to fight back the urge to say to them: "You just wait until your child grows up and doesn't follow the path *you* think is best for them!" But I don't say it. I'm not sure why, but I don't. Maybe it's because I'm aware that unless you actually live the experience that teaches you that kind of lesson, it'd just go in one ear and out the other anyway.

CHAPTER SIX

The End of Life as I Knew It

It takes a while for wisdom like that to sink in, though. When I got home from Duluth, I didn't tell my husband about the conversation we'd had. That was pretty unusual, because my husband and I usually tell each other everything. In this case, though, I tried not to think about what Cathy had told me, hoping and praying the unsettling feeling I had would just go away. So I kept clinging to the fact that she'd told me she still loved her husband. But the feeling didn't go away. Far from it. Instead, it mushroomed into a state of turmoil that I couldn't make go away no matter how much I wished it would.

Over the course of the next several months, we began to get increasingly disturbing phone calls from our daughter telling us she wasn't sure what was going to happen to her marriage. Moreover, she wasn't sure what she was going to do about her life in general. It was during one of these phone calls that we found out she and her husband had decided on a trial separation. I think I still only heard what I wanted to hear, but I finally did tell Aaron about the conversation I'd had with Cathy in Duluth. We tried to comfort each other then, secure in the knowledge that Cathy had gone through many different phases in her life. We tried to reassure ourselves by telling each other that this was maybe just another phase and hoped that the bond she shared with her husband would be strong enough to survive it.

But then the letter came. It was in November, less than two years after Bob and Cathy had gotten married. I remember it was one of those windy and cold autumn days that send chills up your spine because you know it's the beginning of the long winter to come. As soon as I saw the letter my heart sank. I'm not sure why, but I suppose it was because of the phone conversations we'd been having that I felt an overwhelming sense of impending doom before I even opened the envelope.

"Dear Mom and Dad," she wrote. "I am a lesbian." That first sentence stopped me cold. I sat at the kitchen table for a few minutes with my heart pounding before even being able to read on. I closed my eyes and began to cry. When I opened my eyes, it took a moment for me to be able to even focus enough to continue reading the letter, because the writing on the page looked so blurry at first. Once my eyes began to clear, I knew I couldn't deny the reality any longer. There's something about seeing the words on a page that makes it harder to dismiss as I'd tried to do with the talk we'd had in Cathy's kitchen six months earlier. I was forced to admit, as I read the rest of the letter, that this probably wasn't just a phase she was going through. In it, she tried to explain things to us more clearly in ways that one can sometimes do more easily in writing than by talking on the telephone. Handwritten, not typed, on ten pages of notebook paper she says at one point: "I don't want anyone to hurt. I guess the only possibility I have of helping you understand me better is to open up my life to you – but that's scary too because I'm afraid you won't understand." She went on to try and explain everything. In one part, she said: "I'm happy. I know you are worried about me being happy. I'm sad, too. I've been feeling those opposite emotions quite a bit lately. I'm happy because I'm at a place right now where I feel more honest about who I am than I ever have before. That makes me happy. But I'm sad because in order to get to a place where I could live most honestly I had to take a road that involved people getting hurt."

Despite her logical explanations, I wanted to shout at the top of my lungs: "Please, dear God! Don't let this happen to my family!" But I didn't scream out loud. I just sat there quietly and cried.

Our son Henry was a junior in high school at the time. When he came home from school that afternoon, I was still sitting at the kitchen table with the letter in front of me, my eyes red from having cried off and on for most of the day. I looked up to say hello to him when he walked in the door, and I'm sure he could see that I'd been crying. When he asked me what was wrong, I just handed him the letter from Cathy. He stood there reading it, and when he was finished, he said, "So what's the big deal? It's not the worst thing in the world, is it?"

I couldn't believe he was asking me that and in such a nonchalant way. It was a really big deal to me, and at that moment I couldn't think of anything that could be much worse. My daughter's marriage was over, and now she's telling us she's a lesbian. How do I cope with this? I don't really remember exactly what I said in response to his question, but I vaguely recall saying something like "Oh, God, Henry, I've always felt I was okay with people being gay or lesbian, or whatever—but now I realize I just don't want that for my child, you know?" I don't remember much else about that particular day. I don't recall my husband coming home or what was said when he did. The memory stops with me and my son in the kitchen on a dreary and cold November afternoon.

◆　◆　◆

I do, however, regret having said that to my son that day. We would learn a few years later that our son had also been questioning his sexual orientation, and it wasn't until we were in family treatment for his drug and alcohol abuse that he finally found the courage to tell us. But that's another story altogether. He has told me that seeing my reaction to Cathy's announcement in the letter, not just that day but how I acted for several months after, added to him feeling that he couldn't ever come out of the closet to us.

◆　◆　◆

After the initial shock of the letter wore off, we began the work of dealing with the reality of having a child who has announced her sexuality to us. As Catholics, we'd been told that homosexuality is a sin. As a mother, I could not recognize a sinner in the form of our daughter. To my way of thinking, and the vantage point I had as a parent, Cathy has always been the most Christian-minded person I know. The realization that she was now a homosexual made it difficult for me, at first, to reconcile that fact with the teachings of my Catholic background that told me she'd be condemned to hell for all eternity. I slowly began to realize that I needed some outside help in dealing with the situation.

As a family physician, Aaron was aware of the local PFLAG group (Parents, Friends and Family of Lesbians and Gays) and where and when their meetings were, and he began urging me to consider the idea of us attending a meeting. I resisted at first, because I hate meetings in general and self-help group meetings in particular. The way I'd been raised made me afraid of going and doubtful that it would help. How could I confide in strangers when I'd not even been able to tell close family members or friends yet? But I also began to realize I needed to talk to somebody about my feelings, so I finally agreed to go.

Despite the resistance I'd displayed about attending one of these meetings, I was pleasantly surprised to realize that just minutes after arriving at that first meeting I did not feel we were among strangers at all. Here were other people who had been where I was now. They understood in a way that even our family and close friends couldn't, because they'd walked in our shoes. As my husband and I shared our story amid a deluge of tears on my part, we received comfort and hope in return.

Aside from being able to share feelings and commiserate with other parents, the PFLAG group was also a good source for self-help literature and videos on the topic of homosexuality. Books, videos, etc., became extremely valuable to me in searching not just for answers but advice in helping me make sense of it all. It was at a PFLAG meeting that I first heard about the book which helped me and my husband the most. Written by Rob Foreman Dew, titled *The Family Heart,* it is a supportive family memoir about her son's coming out and their family's journey from confusion to acceptance. The book goes beyond acceptance to a commitment to her readers to help them understand homosexuality.

I borrowed the book from PFLAG's library, and after reading it, I told Cathy about it and recommended she read it. She then bought a copy of the book and gave it to me for a Christmas present, the same year that we finally decided to announce Cathy's lesbianism to friends and family in our Christmas letter. As usual, when giving a book for a gift she wrote an inscription saying the following:

> My Dearest Mother, Where do I start in thanking you and telling you how proud I

am of you? I think it's ironic that you intro-
duced **Me** to this book – but maybe that was
just indicative of how much you and Daddy
have grown in accepting my whole person –
so much more than I expected and even more
than I hoped for. I listen to you telling me
about the wonderful people you've met or
have known and found out they're gay –
bonding with them in a solidarity I cherish –
and hear you explain in sometimes vivid detail
the experiences you've had and your reactions
to homophobia, and somewhere deep inside
my soul glows in a connection with you
that I never dreamed could happen. I think
the "struggle" to **all** of us accepting gayness
in this family has made us closer than ever
in so many ways – and has helped us show
each other, and "the rest of the world" what
FAMILY really means!

In addition to the hardcover copy of the book that I keep
proudly on my bookshelf in my office are two softcover copies I purchased and began to loan out to anyone who might
be interested in reading it. I gave a copy to both our parents
that Christmas for gifts too. I hoped it would help them understand things that maybe Aaron and I hadn't figured out how to
explain to them yet.

CHAPTER SEVEN

Life in the Proverbial Closet

Despite the steps we took to educate ourselves about homosexuality, and the journey that had begun toward acceptance of our lesbian daughter, my husband and I did choose to live in the closet for quite a while before having enough courage to actually "come out" ourselves. That's the thing. Ironic as it may be, when Cathy finally had the confidence to come out to us, we started living a closeted type of life similar to the one Cathy had been in and was now so happy to be free of. As uncomfortable as it was living through that period of time, I have to admit that it helped me to truly understand and empathize with all of our GLBT children and what they must go through before coming out to family and friends.

It took us a while, too, to find enough courage to come out to *our* friends and various family members that we were at first afraid to confide in. In fact, we even told Cathy that it was her job to let her grandparents know, mainly because we didn't know if we could do it ourselves. She did so by way of a letter to them, just as she had done with us. Meanwhile, we worried about many of the same things that I would imagine Cathy worried about. What will people say? Will they judge our parenting skills and condemn us while quoting the Bible to us? Most importantly, I think, is the fear we harbor within our hearts that we will lose friends and family because of it. I don't know why I worried so much about this, because the positive reactions from our parents when Cathy first wrote to them and told them she was a lesbian should have helped me to realize that a lot of those fears were without merit.

In fact, my mother-in-law, who is one of the staunchest Catholics I know, never skipped a beat in declaring, "Cathy is my granddaughter and I will always love her no matter what!" This came from a lady who still attends daily mass, is a deacon in her church, and is actively involved in all kinds of other church-related organizations. Despite what she may feel in her heart about homosexuality, she has never wavered in showing her love and support of and for her grandchild. The reaction from my own parents, who both have since passed away, was pretty much the same. I wasn't worried about my mother because I had always known her to be a very loving and accepting person. I did have doubts about my father's reaction, though, because he was what I would lovingly term an "Archie Bunker" type of man. He was bigoted and extremely strong-willed and conservative in his thinking. But he, like my mother-in-law, simply stated "I will always love Cathy. How could I not love my Madame Queen?"

Our parents' reactions should have let us know that the process of telling friends and family that we'd not yet told that our daughter was a lesbian probably shouldn't have been that daunting. However, because of worrying about how people would react to such news, it was a scary prospect for us, and we remained in our own version of the closet for a couple of years. I hated it.

For example, I'd be out golfing with friends whose son or daughter had gone to school and graduated with Cathy, and

I would be terribly uncomfortable about the subject of our children coming up as a topic of conversation. It often did, of course, and they'd inevitably ask how she was (or how Cathy and Bob were, if they were friends who knew Cathy had been married). I would simply reply "fine" and hope they didn't ask more questions. I didn't want to go into the fact that Cathy was now divorced nor did I want to even broach the subject of why they'd gotten divorced. At the same time, I resented how they were able to talk, and often brag as parents tend to do, about their child and what was going on in their lives. Suffice it to say that I wasn't much of a conversationalist in those days of living in the closet.

That kind of living is frustrating at best, so once we summoned enough courage, my husband and I decided to announce the changes that had happened in our family in our annual Christmas letter. In looking back over the copies I've saved of our Christmas letters over the years, I am reminded that we came out of our closet tentatively, taking baby steps at first. In 1994 I simply wrote:

> Without going into great detail we are sad to tell you that Cathy and Bob separated last spring. Thankfully, they parted on good terms and remain friends. They just couldn't stay married, I guess. Our daughter, the "feminist," is quite happy, and as parents that's what we mainly wish for our children after all.

It wasn't until the following year in our Christmas letter that my husband and I decided to actually "come right out" and tell everyone that our daughter was a lesbian. After the paragraph about our son Henry I wrote:

The time has come for Aaron and me to come out of the closet we've been living in for the past two years. While the closet can be a terribly small and uncomfortable place to live, we did allow that kind of life while trying to accept the situation ourselves but we don't want to live this way any longer. Though it may come as a shock to some of you, we've come to the point in our family where we need to let you know that Cathy is a lesbian. She has a partner named Deb who we are getting to know and love. We realize we might risk losing some friends and family by telling you this, but we want to take that risk because of the love and pride we have for our daughter. And life goes on.

Since we've done quite a lot of moving around over the years, our Christmas card list is pretty extensive. As we had done every year, we sent the letter to everyone on the list, and I have to admit it was an overwhelmingly positive reaction from almost everyone. We had long since decided that if we lost friends because of their lack of understanding these would be friends we could survive without because, after all, who needs friends that are that judgmental? (The cliché comes to mind: "With friends like that who needs enemies?") But I still worried about the reaction of other family members since both of us come from Catholic backgrounds. A few friends here and there I thought I could do without, but I wasn't sure I could handle losing family members.

However, the reactions we got to what we really felt was a stunning announcement made that year couldn't have surprised us more. We even got several responses that were affirming and supportive, praising us for the unconditional love for our child that our letter represented. Of course I'm not going to lie and say that that we didn't get any negative reactions at all. We did. In fact there were a couple of friends who could be described as being self-proclaimed good Christians who wrote and said they would pray for us and most especially for Cathy. We even got advice from one couple that suggested we take our daughter to therapy or whatever else it might take to get her back on the "right path." I realize they probably felt their response was a loving and Christian one, but we didn't respond to it, nor are we still friends with that particular couple. Cathy, having been raised a Catholic herself and even becoming in college a staunch Bible-reading Christian, had already gone the route of going to therapy to (as she put it to us when she told us) "get fixed." Thankfully, the therapist was enlightened enough to help her to accept her sexual orientation as opposed to suggesting they go the route of "deprogramming" her. Scientific studies have shown this process does not work, despite what some say. In fact, in 1973 the American Psychiatric Association officially removed "homosexuality" from the DSM (*Diagnostic and Statistical Manual of Mental Disorders*) as a mental disorder.

◆　◆　◆

All of this seems somewhat silly to me as I sit here in the autumn of 2010 looking back over the past decade and a half. A lot of time has passed since composing the first drafts of the preceding chapters. Talking about the lesbian issue seems relatively trivial and even inconsequential to me now in comparison to trying to understand and accept your child changing their gender identity, but that's exactly what was to come next for our family. It also occurs to me at this moment that when our son Henry told us he was gay years later, it was not nearly so traumatic or earthshaking. But by then, our family had come a long, long way.

♦   ♦   ♦

For several years, I thought homosexuality was the most misunderstood and unaccepted minority. I realize now I was wrong. Though homosexuality is still very much maligned, we have at least been made well aware of the *existence* of gay and lesbian people. On the other hand, we as a society are only now beginning to become aware of the very real existence of that part of our society that identifies as transgender.

"Junior Prom"
Me with Cathy - Age 16

High School Graduation 1989 Cathy Age 18

Cathy as the Bride
1992
Henry, Me, Cathy & Aaron

1994
Cathy and HerShe

"Hate is Not a Family Value"
Our Family at Duluth Pride
Festival 1997

Giant's Ridge Ski Trip 1997
Me with Cathy - Age 26

Summer 2000 - Cathy, Henry & HerShe

Summer 2001 - Aaron & Cathy

PART THREE

Mother of Two Sons

CHAPTER EIGHT

The Phone Call

Days that throw your life into utter chaos usually start out like any other ordinary day. They catch you off guard and—a lot of the time—not even paying attention. It was on exactly that kind of day when I remember hearing Cathy use the term "transgender" in reference to herself for the first time. Later I would wonder: why hadn't I paid better attention? If I had, maybe I'd have been better prepared for what was to come. Maybe, maybe not.

♦ ♦ ♦

I'm in the kitchen unloading the dishwasher when the phone rings. The harsh sound of the ringing phone disturbs the morning peace and quiet I always enjoy once Aaron has left for work. Walking to the phone to check the caller identification, I'm not even sure I'll answer it because of all the telemarketing calls we get. But I smile and pick up the phone when I see it's my daughter calling.

After exchanging hellos I say, "Gosh, Cathy, it's so good to hear your voice and you know what? It feels closer than it used to. Does that sound stupid?"

"Not at all, Mom. I am a lot closer to you now, and it's great to be living back in Minnesota again. It feels like I've returned home. Living in Dayton was all right at first. I needed time away to sort

things out after the divorce and the way things ended with Deb, but I'm really happy I moved back. I was too far away from everyone."

"I'm happy you moved back too," I said.

♦ ♦ ♦

After her divorce from Bob, Cathy had had a couple of lesbian relationships. One lasted for over a year, but ended badly. Thinking a change in scenery was the answer, when she got an offer to live in Ohio with a couple of her good friends, she packed up her car and her dog and constant companion, Hershe, and relocated. After a couple of years, she decided to move back to Minnesota and chose Minneapolis because she felt it had more to offer.

♦ ♦ ♦

"How's the job hunting going? Any luck yet?" I asked.

"That's partly why I called, Mom. I wanted to tell you about the application I filled out for a job at the university today."

"Oh? What about it?" I'm cradling the phone receiver on my shoulder so I can finish unloading the dishwasher while we are talking, so I'm somewhat distracted.

"I was surprised to see on the application form it gives you more than just the choice of checking the box for male or female. They actually have a transgender box you can check."

"Hmmm . . . that's interesting," I said casually, not really caring much less realizing why she was even telling me this. Obviously it was some new form of political correctness or something the university had implemented, being liberal oriented as most universities are, in my opinion. To my daughter I feigned an interest that wasn't really there. "So what box did you check, then?" I was making sort

of a joke out of it, thinking that obviously she would've checked the
box for female.

"Yes, it IS *interesting, Mom. I checked the transgender box."*

◆   ◆   ◆

If I am to be completely honest (and I do want to be) I have to admit that this might not even be the way the conversation actually went. I'm not transcribing here. I'm simply recalling the memory I have of the first time I heard Cathy use the term "transgender" as it related to her.

Memoirist Patricia Hampl tells us, "We store in our memory, only those things of value," and I agree this is true. However, we don't store all the specific details—at least I don't. All I truly remember is the gist of the phone call and that I was unloading dishes in the kitchen while we talked. It wasn't until later on when Cathy began to gradually come out to us about identifying as transgender that I knew it had been a more important phone call then I realized at the time. Maybe not the entire conversation, but Cathy's statement to me of "I checked the transgender box" is something I now realize was pretty significant in the grand scheme of things.

On that day, though, during our phone conversation I shrugged off her comment as just being a typical thing for my oldest child to say. Heaven forbid that she should be forced to choose between being either a female *or* a male. Why couldn't she be a little of both? While she was growing up we always allowed her to do whatever she wanted to do—within reason. Therefore, she didn't have to choose between playing basketball or being in the band. She did both. If there were two sports offered during the same season and she wanted to participate in both of them instead of picking one, we let her do that. So these are the things I thought of when she began talking about "transgender" as being a truer indication of who she was.

A comment that Cathy had made more than once to us even before beginning her transition keeps reverberating in my mind. "I don't hate the part of myself that is female. I have never hated being a girl or a woman, but that isn't all that I am. There are some male qualities I deeply identify with."

So the day she told me she'd checked the transgender box on an application form, I thought of it as being typical of my oldest child. I imagined her saying: "Don't force me to choose between one or the other. I'm a little of both!"

Maybe I was just trying to close my mind to the reality of the situation again like I'd done the day we'd had the conversation in her kitchen about her being bisexual. But I certainly didn't think what Cathy had told me on the phone about checking a "transgender" box on a job application was anything earthshaking at all.

However, the rumblings of an earthquake had begun that would once again throw my world into complete chaos. It's like a giant jigsaw puzzle I'm trying to piece together in some kind of logical order. I think that's part of what this writing is about. It's an attempt to put all the pieces of the puzzle together.

CHAPTER NINE

How Obtuse Can One Person Be?

Chronologically, what I relate in this chapter probably belongs in the section that talks about Cathy as a lesbian. The personal writings she shared with us while still in college in Duluth that she wrote for classes she was taking in Women's Studies, the book she loaned us titled *Gender Outlaw: On Men, Women, and the Rest of Us* by Kate Bornstein after she attended one of Bornstein's lectures at the university, and the many talks we had about gender identity all took place while Cathy was still a lesbian.

However, neither Aaron nor I realized at the time that Cathy would eventually decide to actually transition from being a female to a male. When I began to write this memoir, I wrote up a timeline of all the significant things that had occurred since Cathy first came out to us as a lesbian. Looking at the timeline in black and white shocked me, because I realized then that she'd shared not just writings she'd done but writings by other people about gender identity that I have to admit were confusing to me the first time I read them. It wasn't until Cathy actually began her transition to becoming Tommie both physically and legally that I would go back and look at those writings, think about those discussions, and understand their significance for the first time.

When discussing this with Tommie just a few days ago, he said he could completely understand that we didn't pick up on things and he didn't think we'd been obtuse at all. It was a slow process for him too, he told me, not just for us. The writings, the discussions we had were the ways he went about trying to figure out what (if anything) he was going to do about his gender identity. As if to reassure me further, he added that he didn't even decide for himself that he was going to actually make the transition until he was sure what his insurance would and would not cover as far as medical expenses. A gender transition can be as much a financial decision as it is an emotional one in many cases.

In the late 1990s, after Cathy had been to hear Kate Bornstein's lecture at the University of Minnesota, she told us that Bornstein had used a passage written by Cathy in another book that had just been published, titled *My Gender Workbook*. Of course, knowing something my daughter had written was in this book, I immediately bought it. Following the style of using all lower-case letters like author bell hooks does (except where she quotes me) the passage says:

◆ ◆ ◆

the next time i see my mother i'm going to tell her she was right about my sexuality being a phase. shortly after i came out to her as a lesbian, she said 'Cathy, you have passed through so many phases. You pick up something and give it all you've got and it's always just a phase. This is just another one. I should know, I'm your mother.' well, she said something like that anyway. at the time, i responded to her (rather defensively) by saying that i hadn't been going through phases, I had just been experiencing life and learning from that experience and moving on to different stages of my life and growing through the process . . . at any rate, she was right.

◆　◆　◆

I liked that she said I was right, but I didn't fully understand why she was even saying it. Is she saying that being a lesbian is just another phase? What then? Cathy has always been a deep-thinking and philosophical person. The fact that she'd been quoted in a book that delves into studying gender wasn't really all that surprising to me or my husband.

There were a couple of times that Aaron did ask Cathy if there was something she was trying to tell us by sharing with us those particular writings. She assured him that she liked being a woman and had no intentions of doing anything drastic to change that.

In January of 2004, though, Cathy did legally change her name to Tommie Michele, and while it might be hard to believe, neither Aaron nor I realized the significance of the name change until six months later when Tommie began taking hormones. At one of their visits home before Cathy legally changed her name, we noticed our future daughter-in-law, Francine, referring to Cathy as "Tommie" and calling her by that name. When we asked them about it, they downplayed the significance of it and didn't let us know at that time that Cathy had actually been thinking about legally changing her name.

We were to find out later that the main reason they skirted the issue with us at first is that Cathy was still trying to figure out what (if anything) her insurance would cover as far as a gender change was concerned. Until she was sure that it would even be possible financially, she didn't want to make any announcements. So instead she explained the name change to us as being her way of being more androgynous to the outside world. That's the way I would explain it for the next six months, to friends and family who asked me about her new name.

CHAPTER TEN

A Slow Process

The process a family goes through when their child decides to transition to the opposite gender is quite a bit different from having your child come out of the closet to announce their sexual orientation. At least that's been our family's experience. Finding out that Cathy was a lesbian was a relatively quick and in some ways even an easy process compared to making the transition from having a female daughter to gradually accepting the reality that she is now a he and identifies to society as a male.

When Cathy first came out to her brother, my husband, and me to let us know she was a lesbian, it was by way of a straightforward announcement in a letter. "Dear Mom, Dad and Henry, I am a lesbian." Although I believe she tried her best at the time to be patient with us, she also was fairly demanding in wanting us to come to terms with her sexual orientation as quickly as possible. Patience has never been one of her strong points, but later on I would come to realize that whether a person is patient or not, once they've accepted their sexual orientation and stepped out of the confines of their closet, they are, quite naturally so, insistent that others accept them as they are.

But that was easier said than done for me. There's a grieving process I went through for a while. I've discovered over the years that this is fairly common. When a parent finds out their child is gay it *is* like having them die—at least at first. I recently read two doctoral dissertations that were studies of parents who had transgender children. Both of the dissertations pointed out this very fact . . . that parents of gay, lesbian, bisexual, or transgender children often go through the various stages of grieving, just as if their child had died. Eventually, what you discover, though, is that it's just your own hopes and dreams *for* that child that has been lost . . . not your child. Nonetheless, there is a grieving process parents go through in the initial stages.

◆   ◆   ◆

There are many families who lose their sons, daughters, and other loved ones to actual death for a variety of reasons—whether it be suicide, terminal illness, casualty of war or fatal accidents. I continually remind myself how lucky I am that at least I still **have** both of my children and that they're safe and well. How much more terrible it would be to have either one of my sons fighting in a war, or worse yet, to discover one day that he won't be coming back home alive. To have a gay child and, yes, even a transgender child, is easier to accept and come to terms with than to physically lose your child completely.

◆   ◆   ◆

My children are both still healthy and happy, and once I was able to get beyond her sexual orientation, I realized Cathy was still the same person inside that I'd always known and loved.

I've often wondered if parents would still have to endure the grieving process if homophobia wasn't such a prevalent force in our society. I'll admit that the situation has changed a lot in recent years, but attitudes aren't changing nearly fast enough to please me. Despite the increasing visibility of and education about homosexuality, there still exists a large portion of society that sees it as a sin according to the Bible. I think that is probably the hardest thing I've had to deal with—the knowledge that there's an element of society that rejects my gay children, and my realization that they are thought of as sinners by people who don't even know them.

Returning to the concept of the difference between the two experiences, accepting our child's sexual orientation was different in many ways when compared to the "transformation process" we are still going through as we come to terms with our child's transition from the female she was at birth to the male he now is recognized as both physically and legally.

I suppose I shouldn't be surprised that the two experiences have been so different. There is, after all, a great deal of difference between sexual orientation and gender identity. Just as I availed myself of educational reading material about homosexuality, now, in an effort to educate myself about transgender identity, I have done a lot of reading about it in the past couple of years. I hoped the reading would lead me to a better understanding of my child, and it has done that. Many of the books have been memoirs, and almost every one of them makes it a point to explain the difference between sexual orientation and gender identity.

Jennifer Finney Boylan's memoir *She's Not There* was one of the first books I read. A transgender person who was born biologically a male, Jennifer lived as a man by the name of James for over fifty years before finally transitioning to a female. A simple statement she makes at the beginning of her book was like a lightbulb going on for me. She says, "… but being gay or lesbian is about sexual orientation. Being transgendered is about identity" (21).

In other words, sexual orientation is about who we are sexually attracted *to* while our gender (trans or not) is who we *are* (our *identity*) as a human being and has nothing whatsoever to do with another person (sexual or otherwise). That's why I like the term "gender identity" as opposed to "sexual identity" because it helps, I think, to separate a sexual term from what is supposed to be considered one's very identity as a human being. Once I was finally able to see it in this kind of light—to separate gender identity from anything sexual—it became much clearer to me. It's not easy, though, because our society still tends to associate so much about ourselves, our lives, with something sexual in nature. For this reason, it's difficult for most people to separate gender identity from sexual orientation because we tend to think so much in terms of who we are sexually attracted to, even if we are talking about our identity.

Aaron and I have been no exception. One of the things both my husband and I wondered about when Tommie began his transition was whether or not he would still identify as a lesbian. That sounds silly, because the label no longer fits him. A lesbian is a term we apply to females. Since Tommie was now identifying as a male, we asked ourselves: what happens to a transgender person's sexual orientation when they change from one gender to the other?

♦ ♦ ♦

One day when we were talking on the phone, I asked him: "Tommie, now that you identify as a man, doesn't that mean you are no longer a lesbian? You loved Francine before your transition began, and you still love her but now your relationship would be considered a heterosexual one, wouldn't it?" Although Tommie had trouble finding the right words, he did his best to explain to me how bringing the idea of sexual orientation into the matter does make it really confusing since gender identity is altogether different. "But, Mom," he said, "That's what makes it so much more poignant to me that Francine and I fell in love with each other for who we are as people, not just what our sexual orientation happens to be."

♦ ♦ ♦

I know that Tommie and Francine struggled with this confusion as a couple when Tommie first made his intentions known to Francine about possibly changing his gender presentation. Francine has told us she then questioned herself and her sexual orientation too. "What does that make me, then?" she asked herself and Tommie. "Does this mean, because I'm still in love with you, that I'm not a lesbian after all?"

Tommie and Francine were in a committed relationship before Tommie began his transition, so it was considered a lesbian relationship. Tommie tried to explain to me that their situation as a couple demonstrates the importance of falling in love with the whole person—everything about them. You don't love someone simply because they are of the opposite gender if you're heterosexual, or of the same gender if you happen to be homosexual; you love the totality of who and what that person is. The more we talk about it, and the more I read about it, I've come to the decision that all the labels our society uses are not really important. Rather, what's important is realizing that we are all individual and unique human beings and that we're a whole lot more complicated than the binary opposites of being gay or straight, male or female.

Matt Kailey's memoir *Just Add Hormones: An Insider's Guide to the Transsexual Experience* explains that when you change your gender identity, you don't necessarily change your sexual orientation. Matt's primary sexual attraction has always been to men. Therefore, he was considered straight as a woman but is now considered gay as a man who is still attracted to men.

For our child, it is just the opposite. As a female, Cathy had been primarily attracted to women and considered a lesbian. Now, as a man married to a woman, he would be considered straight. Kailey suggests in his book that people then might say, "How can this be? If sexual orientation doesn't change, how could you be lesbian as a woman and straight as a man? You changed your sexual orientation." My answer to them, after what I've learned from the reading I have done, is that he did not—his label just changed. Therefore, with the limited sexualities that our culture defines, as a female attracted to women, Cathy was a lesbian. As a male still in love with the same woman as he was before the transition, Tommie is considered straight. According to Kailey, whether that makes Tommie gay, straight, or something else entirely "is a question best left to those whose job it is to come up with labels to answer" (87).

◆　◆　◆

As I was raising my children in the 1970s and 1980s, and was a stay-at-home mom, I used to watch Phil Donahue who had one of the earliest talk shows that dealt with issues of the day. It was on his show that I'd first seen people called transsexuals or cross-dressers. I realize now, years later, that his show exploited these people and gave the public an extremely distorted image of them. The transsexuals he had on his show were usually weird and unusual people. I'm sure they were meant to shock the audience and increase ratings. The subject of transsexuality itself was often treated with derision and disgust by Phil Donahue. I did not want to think about my child as belonging to this group of people. I know my child is normal, but I didn't see the transgender identity as being normal in any way—at least not at first. It horrified me to think that people would categorize my child as one of these freaks I'd seen on television in the early 1970s.

◆　◆　◆

That's precisely why I wanted to seek out information on transgender identity, and I was pleasantly surprised by all the books I was able to find. It was a great deal of comfort to me to discover that there are lots of people out there who identify as transgender who are quite sane and otherwise ordinary human beings. The memoirists are articulate and well-spoken, and I feel as though I've been educated a great deal on a topic I knew so little about. In the past six years, since Tommie began his transition, I have read over a dozen memoirs written by transgender people. There's one memoir I read that stands out above all of them, and I think it deserves its own chapter.

CHAPTER ELEVEN

Jamison Green's
Cave Analogy

Becoming a Visible Man by Jamison Green is much more than a simple biography of this person's life, and it is now being used as a textbook in Gender Studies classes. After reading it, I can certainly understand why.

Tommie recommended the book to me in 2005 when I first asked him if he knew of any good memoirs about the female-to-male (FTM) transition. I had already read two books about males who had transitioned to females (MTFs), and they were helpful to me in understanding the subject of transgender identity. But now I wanted to read a book written by someone who had undergone the same kind of transition that my daughter/son has been in the process of undergoing. The first book that came to Tommie's mind is Green's memoir. It is a book that sheds much-needed light on the transgender subject for me.

Dr. Aaron H. Devor, professor of Sociology at the University of Virginia, writes in the book's foreword: "This is both a profoundly personal and a powerfully political book . . . a book that brings trans[gender] experience to life and brings it home without sacrificing advocacy and analysis. Yet it is a book that remains accessible to anyone who cares to know more about what it feels like to be trans." As Tommie's mother, I count myself among those interested persons.

The analogy Jamison Green uses to explain what the transition process is like is one with which I was able to completely identify because it has been very much like that for our family as well. Although the author intends the analogy to describe the process of the transition for the person who is transgender, I feel that it's been the same kind of process for us as parents and for our whole family.

As opposed to the relatively simple act of "stepping out of" or "opening one's closet," the transgender person's experience is so much more complicated, Green explains. He says it's more like being in a long, dark cave and slowly finding the way out by one lit candle at a time. When I first read the book in 2004, that is exactly how I felt it had been for me thus far, and I could understand that this is the kind of experience it has been for my child as well. I knew when reading Green's book that I had not yet reached the end where I could see the clear light of day. But with each book I read and each conversation I would have with my child, the world around me began getting brighter all the time.

I want to use Jamison Green's dark cave analogy to help describe what the past few years have been like for me. In reflecting back at the various comments Tommie made and the writings he began to share with us, I can now see how each of these things was a candle being lit, slowly illuminating the cave and helping me to come to the realization of who my child really is.

◆　◆　◆

It is April of 1996, less than two years after Cathy has come out of the closet to tell us she is a lesbian. She is attending college at the University of Minnesota in Duluth and taking a Women's

Studies course in human sexuality. She writes a paper for the course and is excited to share it with us. I've come a long way in accepting her as a lesbian, and her essay is very confusing to me.

It's titled "Identities, Box cutters, and Rainbows" and it's an autobiographical piece that talks about the various phases of her life up to that point.

Although it intrigues me, I don't clearly understand it. In one paragraph she writes:

> *when i was a kid, i never wanted to grow up. i was determined to remain a tomboy. sometimes i'd look in the mirror and i'd think, just for a second, that I saw a boy staring back at me. with my hair cut short…i'd think that i'd be a darn cute boy. i didn't want to **be** a boy, but i didn't want to grow up to be the woman who, i had been learning, other people would expect me to be. when i got my first period, i was pissed. that meant a rite of passage to womanhood. zippidee doo dah. And passing through.*

What? I decide I need to read this paragraph over again and it becomes clearer to me. Okay, I think I get it now. As a newly professed feminist lesbian, she is expressing the outlook she's always seemed to have toward womanhood and femininity. This is the tendency toward "butch lesbianism" talking here, I say to myself. She doesn't really want to "be" a boy. That sentence was comforting to me while at the same time confusing. Part III of the three-part essay is even more confusing to me. She writes:

> *it is the working my way out of these boxes that has made me transgressive. i've passed through identities as many times as i've cut my hair,*

or changed my name. it's an active process of growing, changing, loving. questioning what it means to be a woman, a man, straight or gay. challenging not having an identity rather passing through identity. i don't know where i'll end up, what label i'll take on next. What phase i'll be entering. i'm not sure it matters. just knowing and accepting that it will always be this way is a chaotic comfort. It is only because i have passed through so many phases already in my life that i can so willingly accept the questions before me now, the challenges to my latest identity i have found myself passing through.

◆　◆　◆

It will be several years before this essay really makes sense to me. Now, in the year 2010 as I'm writing this I'm able to understand what it is she was explaining about herself. I wonder if, at that time, she was making an attempt to explain things to herself as well.

◆　◆　◆

After we learned of Cathy's intention to transition to a male identity, I came across this essay one day and as I read through it again, it made so much more sense to me. I don't remember exactly what day it was, but I know it was in the summer of 2005, after Cathy had begun taking hormones. I decided to show the essay to a couple of close friends who were aware that Cathy was beginning to change genders, and one friend observed: "It sounds like she is really confused!" I think back now to how disappointing my reaction to that essay must have been to Cathy in 1996 when she first shared it with us. Not being able at that time to fully comprehend its meaning, I didn't really discuss its message with her. I praised her instead for the poetic quality of the essay and what a good writer I thought she was. I distinctly remember saying to her: "I love the alliterative phrase 'chaotic comfort,' Cathy! You have such a wonderful ability with writing. It makes me jealous." I don't think that was the reaction she was expecting from her mother, but she didn't say anything. We did, years later, come back to discuss the meaning of the essay once she started her transition. First as Cathy and now as Tommie the meditations and journal writings, the songs and poetry *are* the means my child used over time to attempt to figure her/himself out as a human being.

Was this essay perhaps the first candle being lit, way back in 1996? As I sit here writing this fourteen years later, I think it probably was but it didn't help me at the time. Maybe I blew out the light by simply closing my mind to the possibility of what lay ahead. It wasn't until I read it again in 2005 that the candle flame began to flicker again.

Around the same time that Cathy shared her essay with us, she also loaned us Kate Bornstein's book *Gender Outlaw* that she'd gotten when she heard Bornstein's lecture at the university in Duluth. Cathy was really impressed with Bornstein and thought she was an amazing speaker. She expressed her wish that we both find time to read the book because she thought it would help us better understand where she was coming from. I didn't take the time to read it from cover to cover, but I read parts of it, and I began to wonder. I tried not to think too much about it and kept trying to comfort myself with the words she, herself, wrote in her essay: "i didn't want to **be** a boy." I didn't recall the line further on in the essay that says: "it's the working my way out of these boxes that has made me transgressive." Maybe I purposely forgot that idea at the time, I don't know. I think, perhaps, that I was just confused and didn't really know what to make of these statements. So it was much easier to just hold on to the fact that she'd said she didn't want to actually *be* a boy. Whatever all the rest of it meant, that was something that would take some time for me and the rest of the family to discover.

CHAPTER TWELVE

We Meet Our Future Daughter-in-Law

When we went to Minneapolis to celebrate Cathy's thirtieth birthday with her, we met Francine for the first time. I hadn't been looking forward to meeting yet another new partner. My heart has broken a little each time one of Cathy's previous relationships ended. This time, I tell myself, I'm not going to open my heart so easily only to have it be hurt all over again. Although we met her at Cathy's apartment when we first arrived and spent some time together on Saturday, it is the memory of when we went out for brunch on Sunday that is much clearer to me than anything else about that weekend.

◆　◆　◆

We are in Minneapolis to visit both Cathy and Henry and celebrate Cathy's momentous thirtieth birthday. We're also going to be meeting Francine, Cathy's new partner, for the first time. Cathy tells us she has fallen head over heels in love this time. She says to me: "Mom, you'll really like her. She's a real feminine 'girly' girl. She loves to polish her fingernails (just like you) and wear dresses and high heels and she has long, beautiful, curly hair!"

We are supposed to meet them for brunch at Ruby's restaurant near Loring Park in Minneapolis. Aaron, Henry, and I arrive first and are waiting for them outside when I see them walking down the sidewalk toward us. They are both dressed up for the occasion. Francine is wearing a pretty brown skirt and matching blouse and a lovely knitted shawl. Her jewelry catches my eye as well as her very red lips. Cathy was right, I think. She certainly is pretty, and she does have gorgeous, long, curly hair. Cathy is wearing nice dress pants with a shirt and vest plus a leather jacket. With her hair short and the clothes she's wearing, Cathy looks very masculine to me. There is a slight rain misting down and the sidewalks are a bit slippery so Cathy's elbow is out, holding Francine's arm, leading her safely along the wet sidewalk like Aaron sometimes does for me. Cathy is walking proudly, I think, like a man who feels lucky to be with a beautiful woman.

Inside the restaurant, I notice Cathy pull out the chair for Francine to sit down like a man does for the lady he is with. Francine and Henry seem to get along real well—joking with each other throughout our meal—and I'm glad about that. It seems like it makes Cathy happy too, that her brother likes her new girlfriend. Henry told me before we came for the weekend, that although he hasn't been around them that much, he thinks Francine is really nice.

◆　◆　◆

It was clear to both Aaron and me from that first weekend we met Francine, that she identifies as the female and Cathy as the male in their relationship. Not every lesbian relationship is like this, but some are. I didn't think much more of it than that, but seeing how Cathy dressed that day and the way she acted that morning left me with an unusual feeling. I wasn't used to Cathy going out of her way to appear masculine. Although she's never been one to be real feminine, I'd always looked at it as her just wanting to be more androgynous. Now, it seemed it had become important for Cathy to not only look masculine, but to dress the part. I wondered if this had to do with what Francine wanted. Was she more comfortable being in public with a partner who looked masculine? Was Cathy doing all of this just to please the new love of her life or is it what she wanted too? The flickering flame is getting brighter and beginning, perhaps, to light the way.

CHAPTER THIRTEEN

The Engagement

Cathy met Francine for the first time at the end of January, a month after moving to Minneapolis. A few weeks later, they went on their first official date. They went through some ups and downs in their first year of dating where they would break up and then get back together. Although Aaron and I were not aware of it until later, Cathy proposed to Francine in April, and shortly after that Francine moved into Cathy's apartment. From my vantage point as a mother, and due to the rough patches they'd gone through, I wasn't sure that moving in together was the right thing to do, but Cathy seemed determined to make this relationship work. She called Francine her *princess*, and from what I could see when we were with them, Cathy went out of her way to treat Francine just like one.

About a year after they had begun to live together, when they were out to dinner with Francine's family, Cathy got down on one knee and publicly proposed to Francine and asked Francine's father for his blessing. We were not in Minneapolis to actually witness the proposal, but Cathy told us about it on the phone. We had only spent a few times together with Cathy and Francine other than a holiday weekend here and there, so we really hadn't gotten to know Francine that well yet. By the same token, she didn't really know Aaron and me all that well either. We also went through a few troublesome times during their engagement period, trying to convince Francine that we were supportive of their relationship. From what Cathy told us, Francine wasn't used to supportive family members when it came to her sexual orientation, so it wasn't something she was used to, I guess. I will admit, though, that I probably didn't give off very good vibes at first because (as I stated earlier) I didn't want to get my heart broken again if the relationship didn't last. I suppose in Francine's eyes I was probably the wicked mother-in-law to be.

They set their wedding date for a Valentine's Day wedding, partly because they had been on their first date in February. I was grateful that they were both in their thirties and would be planning the wedding themselves. For Francine, who had not been married yet, this was going to be the big wedding she'd always dreamed about. She had told us when they first started dating that she'd never been married, because she wanted to wait to get married until she knew it would last forever.

It was during the engagement period that Cathy began to ask people to call her Tommie, even though she didn't legally change her name until a month before they got married. When they sent out an announcement of their engagement, they referred to themselves as Francine and Tommie. Accompanying the announcement, Tommie also wrote a note of explanation telling people it was going to be a traditional wedding, that Francine would be the bride dressed in white, and she, Tommie, would be the groom in a tuxedo.

The weekend they came home to tell us about their engagement, Tommie told me "Mom, I just want so badly to give my future bride the wedding she's always dreamed of. She's my princess, after all, you know." I knew that she would need our financial help in order to do that, because she didn't have the money to pay for a wedding by herself. I had reservations about it, but in the end we did split most of the costs of the wedding with Francine's parents.

Technically speaking, all of us (not the least of whom were Francine and Cathy) realized this would not be a legally recognized wedding in the eyes of the government. However, in every other sense it was going to be considered a wedding and a marriage between Francine and Cathy, so that's how plans proceeded. We took that in stride as we'd been learning to do ever since Cathy first came out as a lesbian. We supported the marriage and we happen to firmly believe that same sex marriage should be legal.

CHAPTER FOURTEEN

Tommie and Francine's Wedding

It was a beautiful wedding. When they first started talking about getting married, both of them wanted to get married in a park. However, when they decided on a February wedding date, they thought at first that would not be possible. The weather in Minnesota in February is definitely not conducive to outdoor weddings. But then they learned of an indoor park in the city at a motel complex that also had an amphitheater and a hall where the marriage ceremony as well as the dinner and dance could take place.

I couldn't believe how picturesque it was when we got there the day before the wedding. Besides being pretty, though, it turned out to be the ideal setting because most of the relatives on Tommie's side and some of our close friends that came for the wedding needed to stay at a motel, and we loved having our rooms be in the same place where the wedding ceremony and other festivities were held.

Together, Aaron and I walked Tommie down the aisle, and both of us were happy and hopeful that Tommie had found the love of his life. It sure seemed so to us every time we were around the two of them. Due to some of the turbulent times we'd gone through with Francine at the beginning of their relationship, I had some mixed feelings as I watched them say their vows, but I could see how much they loved each other and that comforted me. Francine's only sister was the maid of honor, and Tommie had asked Henry to be his best man. They were the only two attendants Francine and Tommie wanted. I thought as we celebrated their marriage that weekend what a great job they'd done in planning the affair. The flowers were beautiful, as were all the other decorations. The music was great. The singer was a cousin of the bride who has a gorgeous voice, and she sang "Come Away with Me" by Norah Jones. Tommie had written songs for Francine too, and they played those at the wedding dance. When they had the mother/son dance, Tommie had picked the song "I Hope You Dance" by Lee Ann Womack, which is a song I've always loved. A journal I gave Tommie for a gift one Christmas had the song lyrics printed in it at the beginning of the journal, and that was the main reason I gave it to him. Was I uncomfortable dancing a mother/son dance when I still thought of Tommie as my daughter? Yes, a small part of me felt strange, but it was starting to become clearer with each passing day that Tommie certainly wanted to look and act the part of the male in this relationship.

◆　◆　◆

By the time they got married, we were starting to become accustomed to calling our oldest child Tommie, as he'd requested us to do, but that doesn't mean there weren't times we forgot and Cathy slipped out. There were lots of times when that happened for the next couple of years in fact. Even to this day, I might slip up and refer to Tommie as Cathy. The pronouns, though, have been the hardest thing to get used to, and even after five years I still find myself using the wrong pronoun every once in a while despite the fact that it's been several years. Early in the process, when I found it too hard to refer to Tommie as a "he." I would often use the phrase "my child" instead. That worked okay for a time but I've grown beyond that now. I tease Tommie every so often about how bad it's going to be as I get older and more senile because I'll really be confused then, not just about names, but now there's his different gender identities too.

◆ ◆ ◆

Although the Valentine's Day wedding is the date Francine and Tommie celebrate as the day they got married, they decided to make their marriage legal after Tommie was well into his transition and had officially changed all of his identification documents. This time it was held at an actual outdoor park. We were at our annual lake resort where we've spent a week's vacation each June, ever since Aaron was a resident in medical school. Francine and Tommie were vacationing with us. Tommie had made preparations ahead of time with a justice of the peace in the nearest town to our lake cabin to have a marriage ceremony. So one day during that week we got all dressed up, drove into town to a park on the lake, and picked out a spot for them to say their vows. A justice of the peace performed the ceremony. Aaron and I were their witnesses. We felt honored they asked us to do that and happy they were making their marriage legal. Understandably, they still have not told a lot of people about it, so we feel privileged that they took us into their confidence and asked us to be a part of such a special day.

CHAPTER FIFTEEN

Hormone Therapy and Top Surgery

In order for a person to change their gender, there are strict medical guidelines they and the professionals who take care of them have to follow, and in order for Tommie's insurance to pay for any of his medical expenses, Tommie had to go through the steps as set forth by these guidelines. In Arlen Ishtar Lev's book *Transgender Emergence: Therapeutic Guidelines for Working with Gender-Variant People and Their Families* the chapter that discusses these Standards of Care states:

> The SOC outlines five elements of clinical work with clients including: diagnostic assessment, psychotherapy, real-life experience, hormonal therapy and surgical therapy. (p. 45)

Once Tommie was assured that his medical insurance would cover some of the costs of a gender change, he began going about the process of doing everything he needed to do in order to accomplish this. One of the requirements was that he see a psychologist for at least six months before being able to start hormone therapy. I've been in therapy myself, so the requirement that Tommie see a therapist didn't bother me at all. In fact, it was a comfort to me because I look at therapy as a positive thing for a person to do. However, as Tommie's mother, the thing that does continue to bother me is that in order to receive medical treatment that was at least partially covered by insurance, Tommie had to be diagnosed as a person with a disorder—*gender identity disorder* is the term they used. In fact, early on as we started to become aware that Tommie did, indeed, plan to change genders, both Aaron and I doubted it was something Tommie really wanted to do.

In the beginning, we both wondered if this didn't have more to do with what Francine wanted. However, once Tommie was given the go-ahead by his therapist to begin hormone therapy, Aaron and I both assured ourselves that a gender change is not something any person would do for someone else—especially Tommie. Hormone therapy involves Tommie having to give himself weekly hormone shots for the rest of his life. Tommie had been terrified of needles from the time she was a little girl.

After Henry was born, when I took him to the doctor for his six-week checkup, Cathy went with me to the doctor's office. She was five years old at the time. Cathy was standing beside me, watching as the nurse gave Henry his shots and all of a sudden Cathy became violently ill, vomiting all over the doctor's office. Then, she fainted. She continued to have that kind of trouble whenever confronted with having to go to the doctor as she grew up. So I knew in my heart of hearts that signing up to have weekly shots was not something Tommie would've done unless he wanted it so badly it was worth forcing himself to overcome his fear of needles.

♦   ♦   ♦

I would be completely remiss as a parent if I didn't let my reader know here that Francine has always been extremely supportive of Tommie's decision to change genders—despite the difficulties that presented for her as an individual and for the two of them as a couple. Aaron and I are so thankful that Tommie was able to find a life partner who has been as supportive as Francine has been, despite all of the challenges involved.

♦   ♦   ♦

Tommie began his hormone therapy in August and actually started out by using a topical gel called Androgel. By May, he changed to weekly injections of a generic hormone called testosterone cypionate. Since Aaron is a family physician, Tommie came to him to discuss all of this before ever actually beginning the hormones. I usually stayed out of the conversations, partly because I didn't want to think about what was happening, but also because of doctor/patient confidentiality issues. Even though Tommie is my child, by now he is also an adult, and I felt I owed him the respect of allowing him to discuss medical issues with his father privately—especially because of the personal nature of his questions for his "doctor daddy" as Tommie often calls him.

♦   ♦   ♦

By this time both my husband and I had become fully aware that Tommie intended to change his gender from female to male. Neither of us remembers ever hearing the actual words to that effect, though. It wasn't at all like the letter where Cathy had stated "Dear Mom and Dad, I am a Lesbian." It was all very gradual and truly was like Jamison Green's cave metaphor. Each step Tommie took from the name change, to hormone therapy, to his eventual surgery to have his breasts removed were candles being lit one by one and ultimately leading us all to the clear light of day.

◆　◆　◆

Unbelievable as it may seem, I wasn't as upset on the day Tommie and Francine boarded a plane for San Francisco to have Tommie's breast removal surgery as I was the day almost seven months later when I saw pictures of Tommie with facial hair. I can almost hear people reactions. "I don't believe it. Just a little bit of facial hair is what finally forced you to face reality?" Believe me, I've asked myself the same question. But following immediately upon the heels of that question is the thought that perhaps I had been grieving all along. Yet for whatever reason, until that moment of clarity when seeing a photograph of my female-born child with a goatee, I was able to push unwanted thoughts and feelings aside and pretend it wasn't really happening. My guess is that I've been through a fairly long grieving period that gets easier with each passing day.

◆　◆　◆

Writing this in the fall of 2010, I can honestly say that I've finally moved beyond the grieving toward complete acceptance and understanding. But five years ago, when Tommie had his surgery, things were not that way at all. There are several different names for the kind of surgery Tommie had. The specific procedure Tommie had done is known as a "double mastectomy" or "double incision with nipple grafts." The surgeon who performed Tommie's surgery called it "chest reconstruction," and Tommie tells me that a lot of transgender guys just simply call it "top surgery."

If a transgender person decides to physically transform themselves completely, there are a series of surgeries that are needed in order to accomplish this. So asking a transgender person "Have you had the surgery?" is a rather inane question. Tommie has opted (at least for now) to only have the chest reconstruction and does not intend at this point to have any further surgeries.

♦ ♦ ♦

It is November 2005 shortly before Thanksgiving, and Tommie and Francine are taking vacation time to go to California for Tommie's surgery. Tommie has done a tremendous amount of research on his own in order to choose the best physician and location for the procedure. He now belongs to a transgender support group and has gotten several recommendations about a doctor in San Francisco who is well known and highly respected for doing this type of surgery on transgender patients.

As a mother, I'm actually more worried about the idea of surgery and possible complications that could arise from having a double mastectomy than I am about the fact that he will now look even more like a male. As part of the Dr. Benjamin Standards of Care, Tommie was required to live openly as a man for a whole year before this, so by now I had become accustomed to thinking of him not as my daughter, but as my son. It's called the real-life experience part of the therapy and Tommie not only dressed as a male, but he now used men's public restrooms, wore a constricting girdle-type garment under his shirt to flatten his chest, and became more insistent about us getting the pronouns right. Because of all of this, I just didn't concern myself with what a big step this was for Tommie in his transition toward becoming a male. I knew the surgery was something he not only wanted but needed to do in order to live his life more authentically.

I will admit that I'm awfully sad, though, and I find myself crying a lot these days, especially after phone conversations with Tommie. Aaron and I have talked to Tommie on the phone several times in the days leading up to their departure for California, and Tommie's been great about trying to fill us in on various details about the surgery and the physician who will be performing it.

Most of the time, I shed my tears in private or when Aaron's not at home, though, because it's when I'm alone that I feel the most unsure about our decision not to accompany Tommie and Francine on the trip. I keep equivocating, going back and forth between feeling guilty on the one hand because we won't be there with our child when he has surgery and then justifying our decision not to go because Aaron and I had decided this was probably a time Francine and Tommie needed to share alone as a couple. We had discussed it many times, trying to arrive at what we felt was the best decision for everyone concerned. Usually, it's after we've talked with Tommie on the phone. I remember the end of one particularly long phone conversation.

◆　◆　◆

"It's getting kind of late, Tommie, and you have to work in the morning so I suppose we'd better hang up. But Daddy and I appreciate you keeping us posted on your trip and the surgery and all of that. You promise you'll keep in touch once you get there?"

"I sure will, Mom."

"Before and after the surgery, if you can, okay?"

"I promise."

I told him that I hoped he knew we would be there with him in spirit even though we wouldn't be there in person, but I felt at the time like that wasn't enough to let him know we cared desperately about what was about to happen. He said he knew that, but I persisted.

"I mean, I hope you realize that it's not because we don't care or aren't supporting your decision to have this surgery that we aren't going with you. We just thought this is a time for you and Francine to share as man and wife, you know?"

"I know, Mom. And I understand what you are saying and Francine and I appreciate it very much."

We hang up the phone after our usual "I love you's," but I still feel apprehensive about our decision not to go. Does Tommie really understand? He's never asked us to go along so I try to reassure myself that this is what Tommie wants. However, I'm not sure if he hasn't asked us because he doesn't want or need us there or if it's because he doesn't want us to feel obligated to be there. On the other hand, both Francine and Tommie are looking forward to this as a vacation they both need and want not just the surgery part of the vacation. They've referred to it as their romantic getaway vacation, and who wants their parents to tag along for that? So I tell myself it's probably better this way.

On the night before Tommie and Francine leave for San Francisco, I'm home alone because Aaron has gone deer hunting for the weekend. As is usual, during the month of November in North Dakota, there's a cold wind blowing outside that somehow matches my inner turmoil. I'm still feeling apprehensive and emotional because I'm not convinced that Francine and Tommie know we care. Added to this worry is that, despite everything he's done to get to this point, I still am afraid Tommie is making a mistake by having the surgery because from all the reading I have done, I'm well aware of the finality and irreversibility of the step he's now taking.

Granted, if someone decided they'd made a mistake by having top surgery, they could have breast implants, but they would never be able to nurse a child. Furthermore, I also recognize that the therapy required by the Benjamin Standards of Care is for these very reasons of ensuring that the person is not making a mistake in surgically changing their gender.

Yet despite this knowledge and the conversations we'd already had with Tommie, I'm still feeling the need to reach out to them that night, so I decide to call their house hoping I'll be able to talk to Tommie, but it's Francine who answers the phone.

◆　◆　◆

"I suppose you guys are busy packing and getting ready to leave tomorrow. You fly out early in the morning right?" I say.

"Yes, really early. We're pretty much ready to go, but Tommie had some last-minute errands to run so he's not here right now. Did you want to talk to him? I think he has his cell phone with him."

"That's okay. I just called mainly to let you guys know we're thinking about you."

I was disappointed that Tommie wasn't there, but I hoped my voice didn't show it. I'd tried calling Tommie's cell phone already and he hadn't answered it. I know I can't say what I really want to say at that moment anyway—whether it's to her or Tommie. In my mind and my heart I'm thinking frantically, *Please, please don't do this! What if it's a mistake? What if you regret doing it later?* But I can't say those words out loud no matter how much I want to at the time.

Instead, with my voice starting to crack because of trying to hold back the tears welling up in my eyes, I say, "Francine, I hope you guys really do understand why we're not going along with you. It's not because we aren't supporting Tommie's decision and I felt I just needed to tell you that one more time.

"Tommie and I understand that. I promise I'll have him keep you posted."

"We will definitely have you both in our thoughts and prayers, Francine. Travel safely and please let Tommie know I called, okay? We love you both!" I hang up and let the tears fall freely.

◆　◆　◆

Francine kept her promise to have Tommie keep us posted. In fact Tommie called a couple of times a day—both before and after the surgery—to fill us in. I wondered if the frequency of the phone calls were Tommie's way of not only wanting but needing us to be there. We were, just not in person.

Early on the morning of the day the surgery was to take place, Tommie calls us before leaving for the medical facility. He makes sure to give me the exact timeline of events for the morning. At 9:00 a.m. they will leave for the clinic. At 9:30 a.m. they will be meeting the doctor in his office for a pre-surgery discussion. One hour later, at 10:30 a.m., the surgery is scheduled to begin. I asked Tommie to have Francine call as soon as the surgery was over. He promised he would, but as it turned out, once the time for the surgery to be over had come and gone, I began to get fairly anxious because I hadn't received a call yet. I've always been the kind of person that worries needlessly about lots of things, so I tried my best to be patient, but I watched the clock closely, hoping the phone would ring.

I don't remember how much time passed, but I do remember it being a long morning. Once I felt I couldn't wait any longer and was sure the surgery would be over, I decided to call Francine's cell phone just to hear the words from her that everything had turned out okay. I might've acted prematurely, because she said the minute she heard my voice that she had just been about to call. She assured me right away that everything had gone really well.

"I was so proud of him, Mom! He was so brave. I think maybe he was just trying to be really strong for me so I wouldn't worry so much," Francine tells me.

"I'm so happy to hear that, Francine, and relieved too. It's all I've thought about ever since I woke up. It is still shocking to me that Tommie would actually want to put himself through this."

"I know. I can't believe it either and he's doing so good!"

I have a hard time wrapping my mind around the idea of Tommie being so brave. As I said before, this is the child who got sick and vomited all over the doctor's office at the age of five years old when she went with me to her little brother's six-week checkup. All the while she was growing up, in fact, even the mere smell of hospitals or clinics had always made her feel sick to her stomach and on the verge of fainting, despite the fact that her dad is a doctor.

Remembering this is quite a revelation to me. For Tommie to be going through all of this on a voluntary basis must mean he's doing what is necessary for him to do. In many ways this revelation is a very comforting thought. But I also tried, while I was on the phone with Francine, to be sensitive to how she was feeling that day, too, so I asked her about it.

"So, how are you doing, Francine? I don't suppose this has been a picnic for you, either. Sometimes I think it's even worse for the loved ones who are sitting in the waiting room."

"I know. I have the worst headache right now and I was just about to take something for it. Thanks for asking, Mom."

I was sure her headache was probably from the stress of worrying about Tommie. I knew this was a pretty unusual position for her to be in because Tommie is the one in the relationship who usually caters to Francine. It reassured me and made me feel good to know that Francine would be there tending to Tommie's needs during the recuperation period.

"Okay, Francine. I'll let you go so you can take something for that headache. You'll tell Tommie we called? Be sure to tell him that Daddy and I love him—and you too, of course. Take care, sweetie."

"Oh, I will, and we love you too, Mom. I promise I'll have Tommie give you a call as soon as he's up to it. Thanks for calling."

I hung up the phone that day feeling comforted in the knowledge that the surgery had gone well. I was happy too because I'd heard words of endearment from my daughter-in-law that I hadn't often heard up to that point. She'd not only said, "We love you, too," but she'd also called me "Mom" and that's something she hadn't done very often—at least not until a few years ago.

February 2004
Tommie (formerly Cathy) As The Groom
(Aaron, Me, Tommie & Henry)

Summer 2006
Aaron, Tommie & Me

Summer 2008
Tommie - Age 37

October 2011
Tommie - Age 40

Our Family in 2013
Aaron, Joe, Henry, Tommie & Me

April 2013
Tommie's 42nd Birthday

Summer 2016
Me with Tommie

Spring 2017
A selfie of Tommie

CONCLUSION

The writing of this thesis has been a long time in the making, several years having passed since I first set out to write creative nonfiction for my master's degree in English. I'm not sure whether to call them justifiable reasons or poor excuses, but several things have happened since the start of this project, not the least of which was losing my original thesis advisor to cancer. She was not just a teacher and advisor to me, but I considered her a friend, and losing her to breast cancer not long after my own mother had died from the same disease was heartbreaking for me, and I found myself going through a grieving process once again. I found it hard to write or even think about writing during that time.

But ever since her passing, I've always had in the back of my mind a soft yet stern voice urging me not to give up on what she considered a very important project to complete. Though I cannot disagree about the importance of the project, there've been other stumbling blocks along the way that impeded my progress, and at times I found myself thinking I might never attain the goal of completing my thesis. Like I said, though, there's been this gentle yet stern voice not allowing me to simply give up. Thinking hopefully at this point I imagine myself walking across the stage to accept the diploma for a Master of Arts degree, and I know I will be compelled look up toward the heavens (for that is surely where both my mother and Libby are) and thank them both for their part in seeing me through to what I consider a very important accomplishment in my life. Furthermore, the completion of this thesis is only the first step toward my ultimate life goal of expanding the thesis into a book and hopefully publishing it at some point. I want more than anything for this work to be of help to others who find themselves in my position and even those who aren't but want to learn what it might be like to be the mother of a transgender child.

It should probably go without saying that much has transpired in my life and the lives of my family over the years it has taken me to complete this project. As I've been going through all the various drafts of my writing recently, I discovered a piece I wrote one day when I was finding it particularly difficult to write anything worthwhile. Looking at it now, I decide to include parts of it since it will give you, my reader, a sense of how things have changed and continue to change as we continue to travel on this sometimes rocky path of our life's journey.

♦　♦　♦

July 14, 2007 – As I sit down this morning to work on my thesis, all seems right with the universe—at least on a purely personal level. Thomas and Francine just purchased their first home, and Aaron and I are as excited for them as they are for themselves in this, their venture into the adult world of being first-time homeowners. We're planning a trip to the cities to see them and their new home at the end of the month, and we're excited about the prospect of actually staying with them at their house, instead of at a motel, which we've had to do up until now because until they purchased this house, they've lived in a small one-bedroom apartment.

I believe we've worked through the difficulties and misunderstandings of the past with our daughter-in-law. She's even begun to call us "Mom" and "Dad," which makes me hopeful that we're finally on the right track to a better relationship and to healing any wounds caused by some of the misunderstandings we had when we first started getting to know Francine. The last few times we've been together as a family, the experience has been wonderful and even heart-warming, giving me hope we can now look forward to a brighter future.

I say that cautiously, though, because the glass-half-empty type of person I tend to be knows that things can, and in fact often do happen in an instant and all the fuzzy warm feelings are gone. Be it a family crisis, a death of a loved one, or some other such life experience, things certainly can and do change. But for now, I'm reveling in the joy.

So when everything is going so well in all the areas of my life at the moment, I ask myself: "Why on earth would I want to sit down and write about all these things from the past that have been so difficult for me to cope with? Why stir up the pot?" To be perfectly honest, I don't really want to. It is extremely difficult right now to do so, and that's why I have to force myself to sit down and go back to that place in time when things were not only not going well, but were like a living hell on earth at times. Believe me, I'd much rather be on the golf course right now because it's a perfectly beautiful day today, and in our neck of the woods it isn't all that often that you have such a perfect day—sunshine, no winds to speak of, and warm to boot. Weather wise, it couldn't be a more perfect day for golfing or some other outdoor activity. I look out the window and hear the birds chirping and find it very tempting to just quit writing and do something much more enjoyable than this task.

But I fight the urge, because I know this writing needs to be done. Why? Well, it's because despite all the contentment I'm feeling right now in my life, I'm also aware of the true nature of things. I know that, unfortunately, all is *not* right with the universe. Our country is currently engaged in what I consider to be an unjust and tragic war, which is killing far too many of our young soldiers both male and female alike. A war that many of our country's leaders are even beginning to acknowledge was a mistake to involve ourselves in.

In addition to this global fight, and the main reason I feel it's not only important but, in fact, necessary for me to write my story, is because of the transgender topic. Furthermore there's the larger issue of the struggle to attain basic human rights for all human beings. These remain topics that need to be openly discussed and thought about. If there is anything at all that I can do to contribute to our society's understanding and acceptance of all human beings—whether they be straight, gay, lesbian, bisexual, or transgender—then giving up a round of golf on a nice sunny day in order to do this writing is well worth it.

◆　◆　◆

That was how I felt three years ago. I can honestly say I don't feel much differently today with a couple of exceptions. First of all, I feel compelled to get my thesis finished so I can move on to what I see as the more important goal of expanding it into book form in order to try and get it published. The audience I want to reach the most is the lonely mother or father out there who might feel completely isolated and alone because they've learned their child is transgender, and they don't know where to turn or what to do. But I also think it's important to try and reach a wider audience, in order to help educate the general population about people who are transgender.

As for our family? We are doing more than okay. Things have continued to improve, and my daughter-in-law and I now have a good relationship. Maybe it was worthwhile to go through the difficulties in the beginning, if having done so is what brought us to the point we are at now. I must admit, however, that I fear I might one day do or say something that will reopen old wounds so I tread carefully. When my daughter-in-law reads this thesis I'm nervous that reading it might trigger feelings that I don't love her or support her relationship with Tommie. I think that might even be one of the reasons I've had such a hard time trying to finish working on this. I don't want this thesis to be the cause of a rift in our family.

An article I read a long time ago in an educational journal talked about the trouble with memoir writing and the fact that when a memoir is published, the memoirist becomes the official scribe of the family, in a way. In most cases what a memoirist writes are the only family memories to appear in print. That's not precisely true in this case, since some of Tommie's writings are included, but since Tommie's writings are more personal and not centered on family, I have concerns about my position as family scribe in this story. I'm not naïve enough to think that my memories will be the same as other members of my family and I wonder how they will react. Will they be angry or resentful? It's a chance I've decided I want to take.

Tommie and Francine, after buying their house, decided it needed to be filled up with more than the two of them, their two cats, and the dog, so they set out to begin their family through artificial insemination. Even after a couple of years of trying they have not yet been successful, and that roller coaster has been difficult for both of them not just emotionally and physically but financially as well.

Last Thanksgiving, our son Henry announced to us that he'd decided to try and help them get pregnant after all. Although Tommie had approached him about this a long time ago, he resisted the idea for a myriad of reasons, all of which his father and I felt were logical and understandable. However, he'd thought long and hard about doing this. His partner, Joe, is actually the person who convinced him that it would be something worthwhile doing. Henry told us he finally realized (with help from Joe) how badly Tommie and Francine wanted to be parents and how much we wanted to be grandparents, and he decided he was being a bit selfish by refusing to help. We were thrilled for Tommie and Francine and proud of Henry at the same time. The unfortunate part is that even though it's been almost a year since he began helping them out, Francine still hasn't gotten pregnant. I know Henry's decision and the many sperm donations he's given his brother and sister-in-law have been a strain on his relationship with Joe, but they both have reassured me that they are able to handle it because of their deep commitment to each other. Sometimes I really wonder how I could've gotten so lucky to have the family I have.

In the latest development, Tommie and Francine have now opted for the more expensive but more successful route of in-vitro fertilization, referred to as IVF. They have just begun this process and the entire family is hoping this works, especially me. I suppose I've never completely given up on the hope of someday having my own grandchild. As my siblings and my friends have become grandparents in recent years, I've tried to be as happy for them as I can be, while at the same time, I keep hoping and praying that one day, out of the blue, I will get a phone call telling me I'm going to be a grandmother at long last. I realize there's a possibility this might not ever happen, and in that case I think I've learned enough in the past twenty years to know I can always be content to be the grandmother of two grand-doggies and two grand-cats.

APPENDIX A

Following is an essay that Cathy wrote for a class in Women's Studies in April of 1996:

Whose Knowledge Is It, Anyway?

"Knowledge is power." Those who control *how* knowledge is produced *have* power. Knowledge is produced by those who are *in* power. Rational knowledge is knowledge that is produced by and filtered through "the system," which are the powerful institutions that govern our society. Rational knowledge is many times (most of the time) at odds with experiential knowledge, also known as humanistic knowledge, which is the knowledge individuals gain from their experiences.

I don't propose to be an expert on the subject, but I already have done quite a bit of thinking about, and LIVING, the difference between "rational" knowledge and "experiential" knowledge. One thing I have learned is that rational knowledge doesn't have to be scientific. It is whatever is widely accepted as Truth. I know that, although religion is not always considered rational or scientific, much of institutionalized Christianity is widely considered truth in "the system."

One piece of truth which is perpetuated in the system is that *homosexuality is unnatural.* Attached to this small phrase are all kinds of large assumptions/justifications for what this "truth" means and how it should be applied (to <u>every</u> person). Religion is the producer of this knowledge, and it is totally at odds with my experience. My experience teaches me (in other words *I* am the producer of knowledge) that *heterosexuality is unnatural.*

My experience has actually been on both sides of this issue. I believe that is why I can so strongly "argue" my case that heterosexuality is unnatural, at least to me, and to countless others who consider themselves non-straight. I was married (to a man) and a member of a fundamentalist Christian church organization, and I believed (accepted as Truth) that homosexuality was unnatural. Yet even while I loudly professed my beliefs/the truth, I was at odds with *myself.* I refused to acknowledge that I was a lesbian, because "God just doesn't make people that way – it's unnatural." How could I be something that nobody could actually *be,* they could only *do.* As long as I didn't *do* it, it wasn't me, because, of course it wasn't in my (or anyone's) nature.

But through a long and painful process I began to admit and acknowledge my attraction to and fantasies about women. And through a series of difficult and confusing experiences I realized that it *was* "in my nature" to want to be and TO be with someone of the same sex. I remember my then soon-to-be ex-husband asking me "Is it better? This is all about sex, isn't it?" My response came from somewhere in my soul, not from my conscious thoughts, "No it's not better, it's *natural.* It's not about sex, it's about who I *am.* "That was a strong enough argument for me to (begin to) realize that I was, naturally, a lesbian.

My experience doesn't just "appear" to "lose out" in this system. It blatantly loses out, is discounted, is totally invalidated. Though I was allowed to marry the man I loved, I am not allowed to marry a woman. I am laughed at and pointed at and screamed at and spit upon and stoned (with rocks) for being a lesbian. I am told not to flaunt my sexuality, while my heterosexual neighbors walk down the street every afternoon holding hands (flaunting theirs), or I will suffer the consequences.

Sometimes I don't know what to do when I am "losing out." Sometimes I don't do anything. In theory, I refuse to be silenced. That doesn't mean shouting from the rooftops that I'm queer, it just means that I deserve the same rights as every human being does. In practice, I monitor situations and appropriateness for revealing parts of my "private" life that heterosexuals are *encouraged* to make public. In practice I do educational speaking and work with queer youth and attend rallies and have one-on-one conversations with family and friends. I want my practice to always express my theory. But that's not real life.

APPENDIX B

In April of 2007, Tommie submitted the following to a GLBT magazine for possible publication. It is the beginning of the memoir he someday hopes to publish. The publication rejected it, but my hope is that he will continue to try and get it published. I think his voice needs to be heard.

A Chapter: Truth

"What is truth is real"
--Don Miguel Ruiz

I've never lived a lie. I live in discovery of the truth of myself. As I learn about who I am and the world I'm traveling in, I choose to live truthfully. That's an ideal I struggle toward. I've made some choices that have had some consequences that I find I don't wish to be in. When I can, I've made new and improved choices, when the decision is up to me. I've had difficulty letting go of some consequences I can't change, find a place where I can "suck it up and savor the taste of my own behavior"[1] – lie in the bed I've left unmade – accepting that

---

[1]   Difranco, Ani. "Wish I May." *To The Teeth.* Righteous Babe Records, 1999.

some of my choices have ended up hurting me and others. I intend to harm no one – another ideal, another struggle. I've always been, and always will be, learning how to walk through this world causing and feeling the least pain, fear, anger, sadness, loneliness. To be aware that I inflict harm on others is both blessing and curse, a lesson learned the hard way every time. I strive to take responsibility for all my words and actions, even the ones of which I'm ashamed, especially the ones with which I'm battling. I yearn to bring and set forth healing with love and understanding – my utmost ideal, more than a struggle, a war for peace.

To say that I harm no one by transitioning from female to male is essentially true. It is my truth, the one I chose to follow once I learned that part of me. But pain is part of truth regardless – partly due to fear, hatred, insecurities. When we're scared of the truth, we ignore or deny it, and if it won't go away, we may become defensive even to the point of violence. Negative ideas of transgressors of my sort pervade every aspect of society – those who are judged to be outside the boxes labeled "M or F, pick the one that was assigned to you" are more likely to get harassed, beaten, or killed than those who conform to strict gender rules. Because most people don't understand anything that's different than what they've been told it should be, fears and expectations cause pain. Regardless, pain is part of my life because I exist.

I've decided my life's meaning has become learning the most I can, about myself and others, allowing others to tell me their stories and teach me about who they are, understanding the hows and whys, knowing the whos and whats and wheres no matter when, striving for appreciation for each moment, expressing back to the universe what I've learned, not lying to myself, being me all the time. Sometimes that means taking risks. Sometimes that means making mistakes, though that's mostly when I am not paying attention, to the moment, to my meaning, my purpose, my intention. It always means that if I think, "That's not me," then it's time to make a different choice. Certain things about me have taken longer to learn than others. I think that's true about everyone, about many things, no matter who you are.

It was about 30 years before I learned enough about me to know I am transgender. All that time living as a girl, because that's what I knew, all the while encouraged to find and be myself, is not a lie to me. It was an opportunity to learn. It was who I was, and that remains a part of me, how I got to today, who I am. I may have considered myself female from within the assumption that was the only option. But reflecting upon my first bleeding, I remember crying, not wanting it and all it meant: becoming a woman.

For many years, I thought my initial response to my first menses meant I didn't want to grow up, which made some sense in that I cherish and wish to maintain an innocent awe and amazement for simple things, a playful nature. But that explanation clashed with my ancient early desire to learn and grow. Now I can see the undertones of my reaction in a new light. It makes sense that I spoke in my moment of truth, through my tears, "I don't *want* to be a woman." But that's just the way it was, I thought. And I graciously accepted that for a while, eventually submitting my resignation letter to the institution of gender, "I'm grateful for the opportunity, but I have to move on." It took me a long time to learn there could be another way, a direction that made sense to me. I turned my blinker on, took the corner slow and crept down the less traveled road to really take the chance to see my surroundings. I've been blessed with several compassionate and passionate souls who've traveled along, pointing out scenery and helping avoid potholes.

I'm grateful for those who've broken off the highway with me, who've helped me discover my holy ground.

Some transfolk say after transition, "I'm finally who I was meant to be." I understand that, but I don't feel that way about myself. I've always strived to be myself, to "just be me." I lived the first part of my life as female. I live my life now as male. I consider experiencing myself as more than one gender in the same lifetime a gift, sacred. I am more myself. I am more myself every day. But I have always been who I was meant to be.

> when i was little, i played with dolls and trucks
> i hated dresses.
> i took pride in being a tomboy.
> as i grew older, i enjoyed dress-up both ways.
> a prom dress or a suit and tie, it was all drag.
> i wonder how much different would i look
> these days in a dress
> now that i'm no longer female
> now that i no longer have breasts.
> i'd rather wear cargo shorts and a henley any day,
> but I feel rather dapper in a tux
> and i still play with dolls and trucks.

During puberty, I read with relief in *Seventeen* magazine that girl crushes on girls were normal, because it just meant you wanted to be like them, to be friends. In retrospect, it was probably my crushes on boys that more fit that description. Perhaps my nonjudgment of genitals went beyond attraction in precedence of understanding my own identity, connecting on various levels with people for who they are, not just their body or mind or spirit but celebrating all of those things intertwined. Though oftentimes transfolk have stated they hated their body, aside from what I would consider typical issues, I wouldn't say that I *hated* any individual part or the whole. I often attribute my ability to accept my physical female self to my parents, who clear my path to make way for smooth transitions of many kinds throughout my life by always expressing their love for me no matter what. No matter what I wanted to do, no matter who I expressed myself to be, I felt supported. Always I was encouraged and excited to explore a variety of interests, find my talents, hone my skills, discover what gives me kicks and makes me tick. I have no childhood memories of not being able to do something I wanted to do because of my gender. Then again, likewise considering that most of my gender-specific transition has been relatively non-confrontational, unlike many transfolks' experiences with their families, I suppose that's not surprising. Being a girl was the package I had arrived in; it wasn't a limitation.

When I looked in the mirror after I'd gotten my period, I remember thinking I was looking at a boy, at someone who was growing to be a man. I remember saying out loud with some sort of prophetic certainty, "I'd be a *cute* boy," not thinking of it as a possibility, just a fleeting fantasy, dream, a funny thought. I don't remember thinking that changing genders was an option. It was not real. But I wanted to be. Real, that is. I was. I still am. I'm still me.

When I listened to Kate Bornstein talk in the basement of the Women's Center in Duluth, Minnesota, about the concept that there's really no such thing as a "real" man or a "real" woman, only stereotypes of what someone is expected to be based on their genitals,[2] I agreed and realized I was somewhere between, less girl than boy, less woman than man. I wasn't ashamed about being a girl, I liked who I was, but I wanted to know what it was

---

[2]   Bornstein, Kate. *Gender Outlaw: On Men, Women, and the Rest of Us.* Vintage Books, 1995.

to be considered and related to as a boy. I wanted others to see the boy in me I saw. There's nothing wrong about being female, not even for myself. It's still a part of me and always will be. I'm transgendered. I trans genders. I check the "M" on everything and ultimately call myself a transman. At this point in my life, that's who I'm meant to be. I'm between genders, more on the male side, and I like being here. Sometimes, though, I wonder if transition might someday have a past tense for me and question my own middle ground – is it that I don't WANT to consider myself "just male" (which holds merit based on my inner queer activist quest), or don't think I'm READY to "drop the trans" (which lends credence to my tendency to make things difficult for myself), or is it possible that I hold a sense of shame about becoming a man? That I've allowed those pervasive negative concepts about others "like me" to be planted somewhere I've neglected to weed? That if I can't be what others expect a "real" man to be then I shouldn't use that word? I prefer and eventually settle back into a healthy pride and acceptance of a spectrum of possibilities, allowing kaleidoscopic identities – we are all of us complex beings, colorful, each moment presented with opportunities to make a commitment or a change. There are extremes, but there are also betweens.

Transfolk are often labeled liars. I've lied, intentionally not telling the truth, intentionally saying something I knew was false. I've also withheld the truth, a lie of omission according to my Catholic upbringing but a matter of survival according to a queer person. Any time any person lies, little white or big, there are reasons, justifications, excuses, explanations for doing so: protecting those we love, protecting ourselves. We tend to deceive when we perceive a potential threat, actual or imagined. Surely this seems incongruent with living truthfully – to the universe, perhaps, but not necessarily the self.

Transgender existence, before or after any physical or medical changes if any, before or after we understand who we are, is not the lie, rather the socially sanctioned insistent *denial* of our existence is the lie. "You're really a woman," is not my truth. Just because someone else doesn't believe in me doesn't mean I'm not real. My living as male is not a claim that I was born male. Others' assumption that that's the only possibility is the ultimate deceit. It deprives those of us who exist outside the boxes of discovering our truth of living less painfully. It keeps all of us from finding out the truth that gender's nature is not so strict throughout history and people and all things. I am not lying by living.

I have come out to everyone who's still in my life who's known me. I've not kept it from any family or friends with whom I've maintained or wished to maintain a relationship. Reactions have varied, but I consider myself lucky that for the most part I've been supported and respected. Part awareness of stigma and part my right to privacy, I don't tell everyone I meet that I'm trans. Sometimes it's just not any of their business. Most times it doesn't have anything to do with what's going on. But it's always part of me, and in my mind, it's pervasive, conscious or not. Our culture is hyper-gendered, and the bipolar dichotomy of our present bi-gender system makes sure it's always present. For most people, gender is automatic and assumed, habit – they think nothing of it. For those who transgress accepted norms, it's a constant challenge, and we are forced to think of it in everything. It's obviously not appropriate for someone to be vulnerably open with every person they encounter. In the right circumstances, when I feel safe and connected, when secrets are being shared, when I'm compelled to take a stand, I may reveal that I used to be a girl.

I've made choices to make changes to my body that make sense to me. What the legal system of my state and country of residence needs, I've done, properly changing official documents and records, though they offer no guaranteed protection of my right to move freely in the world. They're just a *symbol* of who I am, a representation, a way of identifying me as a unique person, a tag for my toe – they don't define my soul. The hardest part of transitioning has been breaking through expectations of who others think I should be. Again, that seems to me a common experience among not just transfolk but everyone. When we can't get past our own expectations, we crumble. When we let others create us *for* us, we lose our way. When we let others tell us who we are because of who we should be, define our appearances and our actions based on assumptions and lies, we lose ourselves. If we learn our truth and ignore it, we lose our humanity. I've never lived a lie. I follow my truth. This is me.

WORKS CITED

Boenke, Mary, ed. <u>Trans Forming Families: Real Stories About Transgendered Loved Ones.</u> 2nd ed. Expanded. Virginia: Oak Knoll Press, 2003.

Dew, Rob Foreman. <u>The Family Heart: A Memoir of When Our Son Came Out.</u> New York: Addison-Wesley, 1994.

Finney Boylan, Jennifer. <u>She's Not There: A Life in Two Genders.</u> New York: Broadway Books, 2003. (Afterword by Richard Russo)

Green, Jamison. <u>Becoming a Visible Man</u>. Nashville: Vanderbilt UP, 2004.

Hampl, Patricia. <u>I Could Tell You Stories</u> – *Sojourns in the Land of Memory,* New York: W.W. Norton, 1999.

Kailey, Matt. <u>Just Add Hormones: An Insider's Guide to the Transsexual Experience.</u> Boston: Beacon, 2005.

Lev, Arlene Ishtar. <u>Transgender Emergence: Therapeutic Guidelines for Working with Gender-Variant People and Their Families</u>. New York: Hayworth, 2004.

Link, Aaron Raz and Hilda Raz. <u>What Becomes You.</u> Nebraska: U of Nebraska P, 2007.

ABOUT THE AUTHOR

This is RoxAnne Moore's first published work. After raising her two children, she returned to college and received her bachelor's degree from the University of North Dakota in 2001. She went on to pursue a master's degree and wrote this creative nonfiction memoir as part of the requirement for her degree. She graduated with a master of arts degree from the University of North Dakota in 2010. She lives in Grand Forks with her husband of forty-six years and their Yorkshire Terrier named Zoey.

CPSIA information can be obtained
at www.ICGtesting.com
Printed in the USA
FFOW03n1555170518
46623750-48675FF

9 781640 277526